NONE OF OUR
HANDS ARE CLEAN

Bonita And Hodge Publishing Group LLC

BONITA & HODGE

NONE OF OUR
HANDS ARE CLEAN

By

Ralph Thompson, Jr.

Bonita And Hodge Publishing Group LLC

BONITA & HODGE

ACKNOWLEDGMENTS

First off, I thank God for life and the chance to write. The following persons provided encouragement as I pursued this goal.

I thank my family - my mother, Rev. Hattie Thompson; my late father Ralph Thompson, Sr.; my brother Daryl and my sisters Faye, Marilyn and Lynn; my kids Reggie and Fallon; my son-in-law Marcus Henderson and my granddaughter-to-be Lilah; my brother-in-law Donald Grayer; my nephew Donald S. Grayer; the Dupree's, Lewises, Winston's, *et al* in western and middle Tennessee; the Henderson's in Colorado Springs; and friends like Negil and Tracie McPherson, Marcia Evans, Lisa Robertson, and Dennis Klipp and family, Denny and Diana Snider, Roger Patrizio, Sandy and Tim Featherston and family, Kevin Kuhlmann, Gary "Nick" Nicholson, Karen and Simon Willis; Gregg Powers and family, Pastor Kenneth Young, Sarah McCoy and family, and all my former co-workers at Headquarters Air Force Space Command.

I also thank my editor, Shelia E. Bell. She took my ramblings and crafted something readable. I also thank my high school literature teacher, Doris Ragland, for teaching me to "organize my thoughts."

In addition, I thank my church family at Mt. Vernon Baptist Church for their love and support.

DEDICATION

I dedicate this book to the rejected, to those the world deem unattractive, and those who have searched for understanding. I dedicate it to the lonely, to those whose faith has been dented, and those who have run roughshod over the lives of others.

CHAPTER 1

"I'm just saying, Dex. I'm tired of the back and forth, dealing with other folks' expectations. I know I'm a good man, but I don't understand women at all."

Twenty-eight year old accountant, Juan Smith dealt with life in clear, black-and-white terms. If things didn't make sense to him right away, he often mulled over the issue until it made sense.

Juan shook his head as he looked out the window of the train. "Man, I put everything I had into that relationship. I put it all at her feet. Natasha and I dated for five years. Can you believe it? Five years! She told me she was in no hurry to get married. For years she told me she was fine with the way things were between us. Next thing I know, out of the blue she walks away." Juan shook his head again in disgust.

"Time does have a way of passing by all too quickly when you're having fun," his best friend Dex said with his tone of dry humor that he usually exhibited.

"Man, I'm serious. I did things for Natasha that I'd have never done all because I was trying to please her. I loved her, and she said she loved me. I can't for the life of me understand what went wrong."

"I'm sorry man. I really am. But you have to move on," Dex insisted.

Juan continued his venting. "Whatever she asked, I tried my best to make it happen. I should have listened to you. You kept telling me not to give her that much power over me, but like a big dummy, I didn't agree. Tried to be transparent. Tried to be sensitive and supportive. Of course I didn't listen, and it got me nothing."

"Calm down, Juan. It ain't as bad as you state," his best friend, Dex explained. "You just travel in the wrong circles, that's all," Dex thought of himself as an expert on women, even when he and Juan met way back in middle school. His purported expertise didn't always pan out. In fact, he was notoriously wrong about women nearly all the time. "Man, you need to get over her and quit overthinking everything."

"But I really thought Natasha was the one. We had so many things in common. Looks like those things were kinda superficial in the end, huh?"

Dex paused, hoping to change the subject and his friend's mood. "Hey, what do you say we go to Club Frisky's tonight? I hear they have a new band playing. You could stand to get out, meet some different women."

Frisky's was a club on the east side of town. About a year ago, when it opened, there was plenty of positive buzz on the street. State-of-the-art sound system. Serious security in place. Valets who were old enough to drive a car, and responsible enough to not dent one. It was supposed to be the kind of place grown folks would want to come and be seen in. No backward-hat wearing youngsters. No gold-digger women tottering around in 6-inch stripper heels. It was to be a place where the classy went to have a good time, but as soon as the initial buzz wore off, attendance dropped fast. Guess the owners failed to realize how few so-called classy folk wanted to be seen on that side of town, even though it was relatively close to the busy, booming downtown scene.

As Frisky's nightly take dropped off, the amenities did too. Security wasn't as secure. The DJ was replaced during the week by satellite radio. The sumptuous spread of cheeses, wines, and fine seafood was replaced by cold chicken wings and stale crackers and cold cuts. What a difference a year made.

Dex didn't mind the swift changes at Frisky's because he loved the flash and selection of women he encountered every time he went. Juan wasn't as enthused, but went out of habit, boredom, or he was just too lazy to break the habit.

CHAPTER 2

Young Adult Bible Study at Green Valley Missionary Baptist Church was one of the more well-attended weekly ministry meetings. It was one of the things, twenty-eight year old single female, Darlene Brown, looked forward to attending. Tonight, after working late at the newspaper office where she was senior columnist, she arrived at the meeting looking somewhat disheveled. She eased inside the meeting room, hoping not to distract others who had made it on time. She found an empty seat outside the circle of chairs and tried to clear her head enough to focus on tonight's topic.

The ministry leader, an older woman with the mien of someone who had seen some of everything the world had to offer was talking to the group made up of mostly young women and few men. The group was made up of women and men all around Darlene's age, except for the Stephenson triplets who were just a few years younger than the ministry leader.

"God made each of you for a specific purpose," the ministry leader said. "But if you don't have any idea what that purpose is, then it stands to reason that you're living a life of confusion and maybe even loss, How can you flourish if you don't know what you're supposed to do in life? Your God-given gifts are a key part of what you're supposed to do and who you're supposed to be. If God gave you a spirit of nurturing and support, then you oughtta be in a place where you can nurture and support. You are fearfully and wonderfully made, so live like it."

After the talk, the group broke up into smaller groups for fellowship and to share in a more intimate setting before the Single Ladies Ministry session started in an hour. Darlene joined the Stephenson triplets, Candi, Cathi, and Carli. She met them when she joined Green Valley a little over a year ago. The sisters were retired from their careers and spent time travelling and serving the local community. None had married nor bore kids, so they each looked at Darlene as the daughter they never had.

■

"Hey, Darlene. How are you?" Candi spoke first, followed by Cathi and Carli.

"Well, hello to three of my most favorite people in the world!"

Carli chuckled and spoke up next. "How are things going at work? Any more problems with that coworker you were telling us about? What was his name?"

"Bruce. Everything's good. Since he moved to Jackson, Mississippi, things around the office have calmed down."

"Not to be rude, dear, but we tried to warn you about getting involved with a co-worker.

Those things rarely work out. And, when they don't, there can be all sorts of awkwardness. Isn't that right, sisters?" Carli said, looking around at her sisters.

Cathi piped up, "Yeah, she's right. I know from firsthand experience."

Candi interrupted. "Cathi, If you're talking about that principal you used to work with who gave you all those problems, remember me and Carli both told you that you shouldn't have led him on."

"I didn't lead him on. I just tried to do my job. It's not my fault he found me gorgeous." Cathi laughed, folded her arms, as if the principal was right there.

The friends continued their back and forth banter until it was time for them to go to their Single Ladies session. They continued talking as they walked toward the classroom where the session was to take place.

"Ladies, today we're going to talk about how to make over your man the Godly-woman way," the class facilitator stated as the session started. The woman who taught the class was well-groomed and gave off an aura of being quite self-assured.

Darlene spoke up. "Why should we attempt to make over anybody? I admit, I don't have a man in my life right now, but I tell you what, if I have to make him over, then maybe he isn't right for me in the first place. I pray God sends me a man who is already made over in God's image."

The instructor sighed a condescending sigh, then nodded grimly, while some of the others in the class mumbled underneath their breath. "Sister Brown, you are correct. However, before we started this series, it was made clear that there may be parts of the study that may not be directly applicable to each of our lives every week. But we agreed that there was enough of God's direction for each of us that the book and sisterly fellowship together would bring us closer. You signed up along with the rest of us. Now, respectfully, my sister, I must ask you to uphold your part of the bargain and participate with the rest of us."

The group grew quiet and the study leader cleared her throat, took a gulp from her mug of chai tea, then resumed teaching.

Darlene worked hard to remain focused on the discussion, but the thought continued to nag at her. Her own life was far from organized, so how would she take on remodeling some grown man? That prospect wasn't appealing to her on any level. She thought maybe she was ready for a mutually satisfying relationship with the right man, after spending years getting over the disastrous one she had with her college sweetheart. In this class, it seemed such an undertaking was full of hazards. Maybe any relationship at all would be a bad idea. Maybe staying single was her only hope at happiness and contentment.

CHAPTER 3

Two late-model sport sedans pulled up in formation at Frisky's. Juan and Dex got out of their respective vehicles. One was dressed in fashionable club wear with a porkpie hat cocked over his left eye. The other was wearing slacks, a mock turtleneck, and a herringbone tweed blazer.

"Man, I told you not to dress like your dad. These ladies don't want to be seen with an old *fuddy-duddy.*" Dex looked at Juan before reflexively admiring himself in the reflection of his car window.

"If they don't like it that makes it easy for me to tell if I got a shot. I'm not gonna pretend to be something I'm not," said Juan.

"Dude, relax. Anyway, the lights will be fairly dim, so maybe it won't make a difference."

Juan and Dex entered the club. A thumping techno tune drowned out most reasonable attempts at conversation. A handful of couples, and some ladies were on the dance floor for the sheer joy of the music.

Approaching the bar area, Dex noticed a tall lady in a shimmering miniskirt. "Let's park here for a minute. I see someone I know." He cocked his head to one side and slid over next to the female. "Emma, girl. What's up? Ummm, you sure look fit. The gym has been treating you right."

"Don't even try it." Emma looked agitated. "You stood me up for that concert that you claimed your friend had tickets and VIP access to." Emma looked over Dex's shoulder and saw Juan. "Is that him?" she asked with a bitter tone. "Don't look too connected to me. I sure don't see VIP anywhere on him."

Juan didn't bother to respond to her cutting comments. Instead, Dex stammered, "Nah, that ain't him. That dude ended up in jail that night." Dex looked at Juan, winked and gave him a quick high sign from one bro to another. " Anyway, let's not waste time talking about a character like that. When can I come see you again? You know last time, we had a great time."

"No way. The last time I gave you a chance, you spent more time texting than you did talking to me. I could tell by how you hid your phone when it buzzed that they were females. You have no scruples."

"Scruples? What are you talking about? I got plenty of scruples." Dex looked back at Juan with a quizzical expression. Juan averted his eyes, looking at the floor.

"And, another thing. I ran into your baby mama at the shoe store last week. She said you two were gonna get back together and raise your kid." Emma shot Dex a dismissive look. "So, don't walk up on me talking about us getting together when you got a kid to raise. Seems to me you don't have any free time. You better run along, and leave me alone."

9

Dex tried to stave off her rejection with a scattershot approach. "I don't have a kid. I don't know where those rumors got started."

"Yeah, whatever," Emma said, sounding like she didn't believe a word Dex said. At that moment, another guy caught her eye. He had hazel eyes, big biceps and six-pack abs that made most women swoon. Emma was no exception. She stood up from the bar and walked away from the dispute with Dex and didn't look back.

Juan couldn't help but laugh at what he saw. Even as he laughed, he had to admit whatever Emma was looking for, neither he nor Dex had it.

■

As Juan and Dex continued meandering around the club, they crossed paths with more familiar faces. Dex struck up a conversation with a couple they both knew from high school.

Juan found a stool near the bar and ordered a soda. He hadn't had a drink since a near-tragic car accident a couple of years back scared him off of alcohol.

The day of the accident, he had gone to a Happy Hour with some of his co-workers from the accounting firm. It was just after Thanksgiving. He had one too many tequila shots, tried to drive home, skidded on a slick street and his car came to rest inches from a tall oak tree in someone's front yard. It was a blessing that all he got was a ticket and heavy probation. He was flat-out fortunate he didn't do any jail time or lose his job, most importantly, his life. Even now, sitting within arm's length of any alcoholic beverage he could have desired, Juan wasn't tempted in the least.

As he nursed his soda, he surveyed the unfolding scene around him. There were people on the cramped dance floor straight ahead doing their thing. Off to his left, Dex was still holding court with the couple from school while simultaneously hitting on almost every woman who walked by.

Moments later, Dex came over and breathlessly described a possible girl for Juan. "Look over there, man. Check out the chick standing near that female in the Big Bird looking outfit." Dex chuckled and pointed. "You see her?"

"Naw, where, man?"

"See the one in the short red skirt and red ankle-length boots. She looks *gooood*."

"Oh, yea, I see her. She does look good, but—"

"Hey, why don't you to talk to her, while I try to set something up with her friend. Come on, man. Block for me for a minute."

Juan frowned, sighed, and reluctantly agreed. He got up from his stool, and made his way to where she had started dancing. His heartbeat accelerated since he hated dancing, feeling a similar anxiety as he felt before the first time he took the CPA exam. He failed it that day, and anticipated that this too would be a crash-and-burn event for his mental scrapbook. He approached the woman, introduced himself, and found out her name was Stephanie.

Some up tempo electronic number cranked up. Juan tried to conjure up moves based on what he saw on music videos, but every time he tried something flashy it just didn't feel right. He even tried the "Flex and Jump," a nonsensical bit where he would strike some almost-manly pose ever so often, then do a little bunny hop. *Funny*, he thought, it seemed cool when he did it back during college.

After a few minutes of watching Juan floundering around, Stephanie stopped dancing in the middle of the dance floor even though the song hadn't ended. "You need to get some new dance moves, quick. What you're doing ain't gonna cut it." She gave a fake smile that seemed more like a grimace, and started to walk off. "I'm thirsty. Gonna go get myself a drink," she said and walked off.

Just then, Dex walked up. "What happened to your girl?" Juan asked half-heartedly.

"Aw, man, she had to leave. She said something about having an early class tomorrow. She says she goes to Downtown State. Ain't wasting time on her anymore, for now, that is." Dex winked, and Juan knew from experience when Dex chased after a girl, he was like a bloodhound on a trail.

"Hey, how'd it go with her friend?"

"Not good. Just a quick thanks and bye. Gotta admit, for a second it reminded me of most of my dates." Juan mustered a wan smile.

"Look, bro. Don't start that again. I know all kinds of girls who would like to hang out with you, but you always seem so distant."

"Nah, not distant. Just me being' me."

"Well, you being you," Dex added, "equals you being alone. You gotta learn to be a different you."

Juan tried to laugh it off. "Different me, huh? How do you suppose I do that?" A weird silence fell between the two friends. Juan looked around, didn't see any prospects, and decided to bolt. "Look. man, I'm gonna raise. It's cool, but I'ma head to the crib and turn in before work tomorrow. You gonna hit the gym on Saturday, get in some running?"

Dex nodded, and added, "Don't give up on this, man. Ol' Dex will find you a girl yet, 'cause I can break 'em down like nobody else."

"Yeah, I've heard that before." This time Juan found it easy to laugh.

The friends gave each other dap and Juan walked towards the door. Sure, he would like to meet someone, someone sweet, sensitive, and kind, but smart enough to handle her own business. Here he was an educated man with a great career, a crib of his own, no baby mama drama, yet he had no romantic prospects in sight. Juan wondered for the thousandth time, *What do women really want, and why is it so hard for guys to figure it out? Why do women agree to wait in line for a certain guy or a certain type of guy while guys like him go without day after day, year after year? Maybe it was time to give up on meeting that special someone.*

Juan went outside, got in his car, started the engine, and drove home alone – again. As he drove home, he found himself thinking about Natasha. It had been six months, six long-and-boring months since they agreed to go their separate ways. Funny thing about their breakup, it happened with no pyrotechnics. There was no yelling, cursing, hitting or anything. Just the sad realization that they weren't as compatible as they first thought. Neither of them knew how to cope when real life intruded with its stresses and misunderstandings.

Juan thought back on their last argument. It was Christmas season, and as usual he had been shopping for friends and family. He bought Natasha a nice gift, but it was based on the woman she was when they met. She became quite upset that he hadn't paid attention enough to know that she had stopped teaching spin classes months prior. For him to get her spin-related gear meant he wasn't engaged enough to stay in tune with her needs. Once the disagreement started and both parties put their complaints out in the open, there was an awkward pause. As they looked into each other's eyes, the realization was plain

14

as day—they had grown apart, right under each other's noses. Too busy tackling the tasks that each day ushered in, they forgot to take time to put enough fuel into the relationship to keep it running.

Juan thought back to the way he and Natasha first met. He had never been successful in cold introductions, but picking up Natasha's coffee order from the counter by mistake gave him an opening. He surprised himself by striking up a normal conversation, and she seemed to genuinely enjoy his sense of humor. One thing led to another and they spent several hours in the coffee shop talking, before they agreed to meet a week later.

He didn't hound her over the next few days. He let their first encounter breathe a bit, called her at what turned out to be exactly the right time a few days later, and found her as pleasant as their first meeting. They became friends quicker than expected. Friendship kindled into a fire of growing romantic feelings.

He declared his love to her on April Fool's Day two years ago. She giggled slightly, then gasped a bit when she realized he wasn't fooling. She confessed that she loved him too, but she didn't look him in the eye when she said it. At the time, he thought nothing of it.

Almost from the start, they couldn't seem to recapture the fresh openness of their first meeting. Sure, they had good times together. Concerts, hikes, even a vacation to the Caribbean for Valentine's Day–all great memories. But, once past the high points, the everyday moments didn't have enough to help them stay connected on a deeper, lasting level. By the time things ended, they couldn't even muster anger towards one another. Their love died a painless death.

Now, Juan wondered if it would ever be worthwhile to strike out on that risky adventure of meeting someone, falling in love, and having something in common that would build into a relationship that worked.

He pulled up in front of his apartment. He checked his mailbox (more bills and junk mail), bundled the mail under his arm and unlocked the door of his ground-floor apartment.

Walking in, turning on lights, heading for the fridge for a gulp of something cold, he felt a sense of boredom along with his ongoing longing. "I gotta snap out of this," he said. He changed into shorts and hit the floor for push-ups. "Maybe some quick exercise will help alleviate some of my stress."

The exercise made a small difference physically, but his concerns didn't go away. As he turned out the light to go to sleep, he wondered if things would ever change.

CHAPTER 4

Darlene got up bright and early, took a few deep breaths, pulled her long tresses back in a ponytail, stretched a bit, then reached for the Bible on her nightstand. Her mom had taught her when she was a young child to start her day off with some God-time. After a few moments in Psalms, she started to pray for God to guide her steps throughout the day and to guide her tongue to say what He would have her say to whomever she encountered.

Devotion being done, she felt refreshed and ready to face the day. As she got dressed, she felt determined to keep this calm period in her life going strong. It had been years since any kind of turmoil or nonsense had crossed her path. No relatives or close friends had died or had life-threatening illnesses. Nobody she cared about had lost a job, a home, or anything of importance. Nobody she knew had committed an especially heinous crime (though that one cousin in Hawaii who got caught shoplifting was in a lot of trouble with her parents).

Darlene knew enough about life that this was all just a narrow viewpoint. Somewhere, someone was hurting. Someone was broken-hearted or even consumed with evil thoughts or plans. She was determined not to let the foolishness of the world stop her from getting closer to God and realizing His direction for her life in the purest manner she could.

She made the 20-minute drive to work in a breeze. At the office, she changed from patent leather pumps to the pair of sneakers she kept underneath her desk because she did so much walking throughout the large office building.

Darlene specialized in community issues, with an occasional dabble in sports-related topics. She had been a journalism and communications major in college, with a stint on the school's tennis team. Although she was never world-class, she deeply enjoyed the competition. That part of her personality stayed intact long after her playing days ended. Not only did she spend time instructing young girls in the sport, she remained an avid player in several senior tournaments around town. Although she knew how to carry herself in a graceful, demure way, the spirited fight of a competitor lingered just below skin-level.

After she finished her rounds, Darlene returned to her office and fired up her work computer. She scanned several of her favorite links for insight or a possible topic to comment about. Usual pop-ups came forth–an athlete causing a ruckus on the streets, another athlete penniless not two years after his playing days ended. Still another athlete complaining about a lack of respect. She sighed, tried to fight off the boredom and disgust of the sports area, and shifted focus to what was going on out on the streets of her city.

In that topic, there were different titles, but the same old self-centered, wrong-headed thinking. Bankers embezzling from financial organizations. Transit workers threatening to go on strike while the city threatened to lock them out from work. Kids failing in state-mandated assessment testing. Darlene shook her head at the various situations. *Plenty to write about,* she thought, *but all of it bad.* She wondered in the short term where this world was headed. So much "grab for me" going on, but not a lot of thought for unintended impacts and consequences. She closed her office door to mull over her options. It was Friday and she had a 4pm deadline for an 800-word op-ed piece. She couldn't spend too much time mulling.

After working on the op-ed piece for over an hour, Darlene shook her head, rolled her eyes to the ceiling, and got up from her desk to go get a bit of fresh air. The roof of her office building had several decorative pieces of outside furniture with a bar set-up for occasional parties, and a small, secluded smoking area.

Smokers would often treat it as a quick getaway during the work day. Every couple of years, Darlene would stumble across some clandestine office romance taking place off in the corner, which would lead to the obligatory "No Office Romance" memo being sent out to the work force. Others would go up to read and relax. Some even brought their Bibles up there to study or minister to one another. The view to the east especially was breathtaking, and an easy way to appreciate the power and creativity of the Lord.

Darlene went up there mostly to clear her head. She had been writing about city cutbacks and how the decrease in city fire department coverage could lead to tragedy sooner rather than later. She had gotten off to a good start with plenty of facts at her disposal. But, she hit a mild form of writer's block. She saw herself use the same clichés and stock phrases she and her contemporaries used repeatedly. She soon got angry with herself for leaning towards the path of least resistance in her writing, as if she was "mailing in" a column.

She knew God had given her a certain gift with the written word, but she also knew that any God-given gift could go away if one didn't use the gift for His purpose. She worked hard at putting Godly principles in her work without the overt Bible-thumping from which some people recoiled. The last few years she had gotten pretty good at it. She had even received letters and e-mails from readers who told her how much they appreciated her common sense approach to the city's various ills. Little did most of them know that the guiding principles behind her written viewpoint were Biblically sound. She got some credit, but more importantly she was feeding the community Godly principles without them directly knowing it.

CHAPTER 5

Dex finished his morning workout and headed to the shower. He loved basketball as a cardio workout, but frankly he was horrible at it. He played for years, but never on formal teams. His game was a classic case of learning the wrong way to do something, then repeating that wrong way for years. For example, he never learned to use his left hand for anything on the court. He continually dribbled with his head down, infuriating his teammates in pick-up games as well as formal league competition. He took bad shots at wrong times, and nearly always forced the fanciest dipsy-doo pass he could conjure instead of sharing the basketball.

What kept him viable on the court was a rare level of physical capability. He was usually the fastest player on the floor whenever he played. And, though he was not quite six feet, he had longer-than-normal arms and an impressive vertical leap. He would only go right with the ball, but when trapped by defenders he could out leap all but the tallest opponents. He never looked up when he dribbled, but with his speed he could turn the corner and get around a defender in an instant. The bad shots he took sometimes went in. The fancy passes he threw sometimes met their targets in mid-stride for some of the most astonishing plays seen in their favorite gyms. In true Dex fashion, he spent scant time dwelling on the whys and hows of how he got to this point. He just lived out his life.

Dex suspected opponents and teammates alike didn't respect his game on the floor and in life. He was bound and determined to show the world that he was the best at whatever he put his mind to. His high school teachers, coaches and even peers at different times said if he ever got a clue about what he was doing, he would be unstoppable. Dex thought he was already.

In another part of the gym, Juan took a break from his lifting session, and ran into Dex at a water fountain in the gym's lobby. "You win?" Juan asked his friend.

Dex chuckled. "Man, if those guys would only get me the ball more, we'd still be on the floor. Buckets, man. I'm about nothin' but buckets."

Juan shook his head, only slightly exasperated. "I've played with you before, remember? I've been on your team – one step past the half-court line and you jack up shots."

"Yeah, man. But, how many of those have you seen me hit? You know I'm good for it."

"I've seen you hit three. That one in high school."

Dex smiled at the memory. "That was sweet, wasn't it? A couple of girls I met after that game still call me and talk about that, among other things." He punctuated with a wink and a smirk.

"The one in intramurals against that team of football players."

"I got fouled on that one. Your boy, that ref, saw the contact and never called it. Shoulda been a four-point play."

"And the one last week that looked like luck?" Juan said, followed by a light chuckle.

"Man, that wasn't luck. My form was pure. I hit the square on the backboard, softly of course. 'Cause I got touch from out there."

Juan couldn't help but laugh. No matter the circumstance, Dex carried that complete assurance that whatever he attempted, it would work out right. Juan wouldn't want to admit it to his buddy, but he hated himself for not having that level of boldness for even one thing, let alone everything.

Dex took another sip of water from the fountain, wiped his mouth, and walked back towards the gym. He looked over his shoulder at Juan. "Dude, you think way too much. Once in a while in your life, you oughtta launch a shot like I do. Think of what you might gain from going for it. Although, you can never do it with the flair ol' Dex possesses." Dex cackled as he opened the door to the basketball court.

Juan could hear Dex yell, "A'ight, I got next. Who want to run on my squad?"

■

Juan finished his lifting session and worked his way to the locker room for a shower. As he removed his sweaty shorts and shirt, he heard two guys talking small talk mostly: kids, bills, free time activities that were scarcer as the years went by. Juan wasn't actively eavesdropping, but he heard them mention pick-up hoops. By their discussion, he could tell the two guys had been on the floor with Dex earlier.

The first one sounded older and spoke with a slow cadence as if he was reluctant to let his words get ahead of his thoughts. "Man, running with those younger cats feels good, but afterwards I can tell my best years are behind me."

The second one had a higher-pitched tone. "I know what you mean. That one kid, the one who wouldn't shut up? Man, he was quick as a blink. Had no idea where he was going."

They both laughed a bit. "Remember when we were that energetic? All thrust, no vector at all? We didn't know how out of control we were. I would love to have that level of energy today. Put that with a grown man's wisdom, you could really do some things."

The second man added, "Yeah, you could really cover some ground. Guess it's just another reminder of how the years race by," he added.

The first man agreed. "Yeah, I look back and wish that someone would have told me how the days melt away, and much too fast for my taste. The things I would have done differently if I had known. I think my marriage would be stronger. My walk with God would have been much more fruitful and satisfying."

Juan heard the two gather their belongings, offer farewells to one another, open the locker room door and continue their conversation out in the hallway. He felt a bit embarrassed to have eavesdropped, but he didn't quite connect to their concern. After all, he was a young man with many years ahead of him to learn, to grow, and figure out his own path. Maybe random old dudes had those concerns as their lives moved into the so-called golden years. Juan felt his best years were yet to come. Why worry now about getting older?

Juan got showered, dressed, and left the locker room. This time, Dex was coming out of the basketball gym at the same time, fresh from another game.

"Bro, I am burnt. Them cats, man, they don't wanna win. They know I need the ball in my hands to create winning. They'll learn. For now, I'm gonna get up out of here, get cleaned up and hit the streets! You in?"

"Nah, not too fired up about it this time. Have fun, though."

"You got it, man." Juan thought for a beat. " You alright, man or are you getting in one of your 'I need to be alone with my thoughts' kind of moods?"

"Just feeling a bit run down, that's all. I know you'll have a great time, though."

"Man, since you left your teens, you've become soooooo serious. You need to laugh, lighten up, ya know?"

"I've always been serious. You know that."

"Well, I'm the great time, man. Wherever I am, that's where the party is."

"Yeah, Dex. I know." Juan shook his head and laughed a bit. " Don't tear up the town too much, alright? Leave some for the rest of us."

Juan shook hands with his friend and headed out the door. It felt like one of those coming of age moments. He knew he never needed to set foot in a club again. He wondered why he ever did it in the first place. He had never really had a good time any of the times he went previously. Never pulled a girl out of a club that he wanted to spend long-term time with. Never felt the day after that the hangover was worth it. Juan felt a light feeling, like a breeze was blowing at his back. Like something musty and stale was blown out of his life.

CHAPTER 6

Sunday came with a bright sunrise, not a cloud in the sky. One of those brilliant blue skies one sees in early fall. The kind of sky that makes a person want to drop out from life and spend the day just staring at the expansive swath of color above. The sunlight reflected off the tall white spire of the church on the corner.

Green Valley Missionary Baptist Church sat at the corner of Oak Street and 17th Avenue, just north of downtown. The church's name seemed like a misnomer, since there was little green and certainly no valley at its present site.

The church was founded in a bedroom community just west of the city. That area, Green Valley, was a little oasis in the midst of helter-skelter growth. But, over time, many residents moved from Green Valley into the city proper. Other members, already city residents, felt that especially in the winter it was too difficult to navigate the incline coming into or leaving Green Valley. So, after much prayer and acrimony, the barest of majority vote decided to shop for a new facility in the city. Some long-time members angrily revoked their memberships, saying that the fellowship would lose something dear in the move. Others rejoiced that they wouldn't have to skid down a hill nearly every Sunday in the winter. For those who quit, God sent others to fill the void.

One such person was the superintendent of the Sunday School program. He was a tall man, ramrod straight. A retired U.S. Air Force Chief Master Sergeant that carried himself like he expected to be recalled to active duty at any moment. Everyone knew of him, but so few people knew his real name, which was Roberto Clarke. Mostly everyone called him, "The Chief."

The Chief opened Sunday School with a short devotion, read a few scriptures, and then dismissed the students to their various age appropriate classes. Juan came in late, and wasn't sure where he was supposed to go. It was his first time at Sunday School in years, and it appeared to him that procedures had changed quite a bit.

"Young brother, you look slightly disoriented," The Chief said as Juan stood at the door looking confused. "You can join the Young Adults class if you're between the ages of eighteen to thirty."

"Thank you," Juan answered.

"You can follow this lady right here." The Chief pointed at an attractive, slim, athletic-looking female dressed in a wine-colored two piece suit.

"Hi, I'm Darlene. Darlene Brown," she introduced herself to Juan.

"Hello, Darlene. My name is Juan Smith."

She extended her hand out to Juan. "It's nice to meet you, Juan. I guess you can say that most of us don't ask questions, we just follow The Chief's direction." She smiled and so did Juan.

Darlene led Juan down the main hallway to the classroom area. Third door on the left, she opened the door and ushered him inside. Around a large rectangular table sat ten or so people, all who looked to be around Juan and Darlene's age. Their collective body language suggested an easy familiarity. They were visiting in the moments before class started, but stopped to greet Juan as he found an open chair.

The class Juan was in dealt with how believers should handle the good times. It was a lesson Juan rarely, if ever, heard from any preacher or teacher. Finding out that God wanted him to handle both good and bad times with the same thankfulness was something that struck a chord with him.

■

Juan left Sunday School feeling more connected to people than he had in a long time. Because it had been years since he attended Sunday School, he had forgotten how much it made him feel spiritually energized.

Growing up, Juan went to Vacation Bible School every summer, and went to Sunday school more often than not. He'd heard the Word of God, could repeat a few Scriptures, but he wasn't fully committed to living a Godly life every minute of the day. His prayer life was spotty at best, praying when he wanted something. When he entered college, he used studying as an excuse not to go to church.

At this point in his life, Juan contemplated getting active in church again. He knew his spirit was lacking something. He needed to acknowledge it and do something about it, but all those Saturday nights hanging out with Dex normally left him dragging on Sunday mornings. He gradually went from showing up on time, but too sleepy to pay attention to showing up late, scrambling to catch up, to showing up midway through service, but sitting in the parking lot until the actual sermon started.

Such a small thing – cutting loose and cutting up while running the streets every Saturday night. He had long stopped actually enjoying the club scene, but went out of habit, inertia, or sheer boredom. *Everyone else seems to have a good time*, he rationalized. *Maybe it's me who needs to loosen up*. But the more he tried it, the less engaged he felt. He often wondered why he seemed to be out of sync with his few friends and acquaintances. Even the work-related happy hours didn't hold much pull over him.

A few years ago, Juan thought he was having fun, getting silly drunk and carrying on at this this bar or that party. He thought hangovers were just the price to pay for a good time. As the hangovers accumulated, and the cash flew out of his wallet, he had more and more Sunday mornings with nothing to show for his Saturday nights but a pounding headache and a pocketful of bar receipts.

Now, as he walked out of church and into the brilliant sunshine, he felt unburdened, clearer than he had felt in months. As he stood out in the parking lot for a few minutes after Sunday service, he waved at a few passersby's and exchanged with a couple of guys promises to get together for coffee or to hang out. Juan didn't have a lot of close friends, and maybe thought he didn't need a lot. But, Dex's lifestyle seemed increasingly unsatisfying, chasing one more woman, in one more club. That lifestyle just wasn't what Juan wanted anymore. He started to realize that there had to be more to his life. Deep in his spirit he felt that God had something more lasting for him. For the first time, he felt there was something that he lacked in his current way of thinking and living.

CHAPTER 7

Darlene left her Sunday School class feeling a little bewildered. The planned lesson was covered as normal, but the conversation this time veered off into relationships, which always made her somewhat uncomfortable. Many opinions were offered as to why some relationships worked and others failed miserably.

Some of the ladies in the class took the literal Biblical view, with the man being the spiritual head of the house. Others inserted their personal experiences and heartbreak when a man wouldn't take on that responsibility, or if there wasn't a man around, period. Still others felt that each person was on their own for spiritual growth, and that God would provide that fire for one to make a relationship flower.

Darlene had little to say. Almost thirty years old, and she had never been in a satisfying, long term relationship. Even now, as a working adult, she didn't have to fight off guys because there were none persistently trying to get her attention.

In her past, she often worried about it. She was always presentable, but never seemed to be the "it girl" guys around her were looking for. In the years when baby fat was all the rage, she was too fit. When near-anorexic figures were sought-after, she was too muscular. Coupled with the fact that money was always tight and she couldn't always afford the latest fashions, she never stood out as a well-dressed girl. However, she never let it get to her, never worried about wardrobe issues.

Over the years, she evolved. She got used to the lack of attention and moved out on the path of serving God. He had provided her spirit and soul the comfort His word promised. It left people around her somewhat perplexed because she didn't act like everyone else. Added to that, she wasn't a girly girl.

As she continued her gradual disconnection from the class discussion, she thought about the guy she escorted to the other classroom. In some weird way, he reminded her of herself when she first joined Green Valley, walking around with a bit of confidence but no real clue about what was in store regarding spiritual maturity. She wasn't necessarily attracted to him. She thought, *Ok, another believer. Maybe another person who can help strengthen this congregation as we all head towards God's Kingdom.*

She caught herself drifting and forced herself to reconnect with the class. She figured making a comment would help.

"We spend a lot of time in class talking about relationships, and I get it. Men and women don't think alike. It takes work to make relationships work. I get it. I really do. Now, can we please move on to something else?" Darlene looked a bit sheepish after she vented, as if she was even embarrassed to admit she felt perturbed with the discussion.

Candi took some time to mull over what Darlene confessed. "Did you ever consider that in working out relationships with one another on earth that we can get our relationships with God a little more right? Maybe we can discover what makes us succeed or fail in our earthly relationships. Maybe you've already learned this lesson, but what about those in here who haven't yet?"

Now it was Darlene's turn to sit quietly and mull over what she had heard. Was she being too self-absorbed to really relate to what others were seeking?

"Darlene, think about what God may be trying to tell you when you fellowship with others who are trying to find their way. They may be behind you on this road, but they too want to get there. They also want to do right by God's will in their lives. Maybe God is showing you something about your spirit when you respond like you just did. Never underestimate the impact a kind or supportive word can have on another."

When Sunday School class ended, the ladies prayed in closing and went their separate ways.

After a peaceful drive home, Darlene parked her car, went inside, and changed clothes. Soon, she was in the basement of her house, finishing up a yoga session before she prepared for work the next day. The discussion

34

from earlier still weighed on her mind. Had she been so unreachable and unrelatable? Did she really have little idea what maintaining a relationship meant?

She got up from her yoga mat on the floor and headed to the shower in her master bedroom. With every step, she prayed to God. "Lord, please give me the guidance and wisdom to do better in maintaining relationships. I have glossed over and run by people so much, thinking I was helping when in reality maybe I did more harm than good."

■

Juan no sooner got back to his apartment when his cell phone rang. It was Dex.

"Wassup, man? I missed you at the club last night."

"I went to church today. I just got back to the crib."

Dex chuckled a bit. "I did that church thang a while ago. I must've picked the wrong one, because three sermons in a row were about money. "Give, give, give, give in Jesus' name!" Dex cracked himself up at his attempt at humor. Dex always cracked himself up.

"They seem like a good bunch at Green Valley. Lots of folks there seem to know the Word, I'll give 'em that. I'm looking forward to going back. In fact, you oughtta meet me there sometime. Would do you some good, you know?" Juan chuckled.

"I take a dim view of anyone or any organization whose initial contact or sole purpose appears to be a perpetuation of their own organism." Dex paused for effect. "How'd ya like that statement, Mister Cee-Pea-A?"

Juan couldn't help but laugh at Dex's attempt to sound dignified and erudite. "Alright, Mister Well-Read. I got it. Anyway, this church isn't like that at all. The Sunday School lesson and sermon were on point. I followed along, and the teachings seemed to be sound, jibed with the Bible. And the people, well—"

Dex jumped in. "You mean the women, don't cha?"

"Nah, not just the women. Everybody there seemed friendly but purposeful. Not there just to show off the suit or car they just got. It was genuine, heartfelt praise and worship. Been a long time since I've been in a church like that. Folk of nearly all ages, all backgrounds, including our age. Almost too good to be true."

Dex was speechless for just a moment.

"Dex? You there?"

"Yeah, I'm good. Just listening. Keep going."

"I think I'm gonna join next week. You oughtta come out. Not just to see me–I'm not putting on a show for you or anyone. But, just to see what a good church should operate like."

Dex thought for a moment. "Yeah, I may drop in sometime, check it out. You can introduce me to some of the honeys there. I read about how churches can be a great place to mingle. Been a long time since I went out with a good church girl."

"That ain't the reason to show, man."

"I know, I know. Just kiddin'.' I'll come out some time. Just can't say when, that's all."

"I've heard that before, man. Don't mess around with this. I tell ya, something struck me on the inside. It might make a difference for you, too."

As Juan hung up, he realized something about the words he'd just uttered. Maybe it was like others had mentioned when he was younger. Maybe there was something about this Holy Spirit thing after all. Maybe God had good intent for his life, something different and useful.

Juan joined Green Valley the following Sunday under "Christian Experience."

CHAPTER 8

The next few months flew by, and Juan became a regular attendee at Green Valley. Several men in his class invited him to join them in their ministry of mentoring teen boys on abstinence, avoiding drug use and other issues, and Juan accepted. Although not having a lot of experience in helping others, he paid close attention to them. He even surprised himself by stepping up with an anecdote or comment during some of the mentoring sessions. The brothers he studied with got to know him, and he felt more connected than ever.

One thing that didn't flourish was his friendship with Dex. It became more than just Juan not clubbing on Saturday nights. Juan changed the times he hit the gym, since his usual gym time often conflicted with weekend fellowship opportunities at church.

Dex called a few times to meet Juan after work, for old time's sake. The calls turned into phone tag, then occasional e-mails. Before long, it had been weeks since the two friends talked.

On the other side of the friendship, Dex found himself at a bit of a personal crossroads. He wasn't built for long-term commitments for anything, or so he told himself. He liked the free-wheeling, hedonistic life he had built for himself. It was even more fun when he had a sidekick with whom to share those adventures.

Now with Juan busy with church stuff, Dex wondered how things would play out. He decided to meet up with Juan at one of the Saturday morning Bible studies. It was, in a word, disastrous.

Dex came in being Dex. Juan had told him earlier where the group met. Dex walked in late, dressed like a hip-hop guy fresh off of a video. Fancy warm-up suit. Ball cap cocked to the side. Fake gold chains. Brand new kicks. Talking smack like he was fresh off the streets or fresh out of prison.

When one of the fellas mentioned how God had delivered him from whore mongering, Dex snickered and made a wisecrack. When another brother made statements about forgiveness, Dex bragged loudly about how he held grudges "for as long as it takes," although he had no definition for what "takes" actually meant. In short, Dex made a fool of himself, and was a complete distraction.

When the group finished their lesson, they linked hands in a circle, and prayed a closing prayer. Included was praying for Dex, that he might find clarity of purpose in his own life. Then a strange thing happened. All of the men in class thanked Dex for coming out, exchanged phone numbers, e-mail addresses, and encouraged him to come again.

Juan fully expected the men's group to put on a fake greeting and privately hope Dex never returned. It was a real eye-opening lesson for Juan. He approached Roberto in the parking lot a few moments later.

"Roberto, I wanna apologize for my friend. Normally he's pretty personable, not quite that over-the-top. This was a side of him I rarely see. He is confident, sure."

Roberto thought a moment, as if deciding exactly how to respond. "Dex is an interesting, yeah, that's it, interesting fella. He seemed nervous, and worked hard to hide it. What exactly have you told him about us, about our fellowship?"

Juan mentioned how he really looked up to the men in the group, their spirituality and insight and the hard-earned wisdom each of them possessed. He was impressed by their diligence to study God's word, and how that came through in each man's demeanor, and how the brothers were consistently prepared every week to cover the lesson.

Roberto contemplated Juan's words. "I think I understand what happened. Dex wanted to put his best foot forward, but at the same time show what makes him special. Ultimately, he may have felt a little out of place with us, and wanted to show us his outgoing side. He may have felt unprepared to speak on spiritual matters, but wanted to speak on what he thought he knew about life. You know us guys; a lot of us try to use humor to deflect when we are in situations that expose our weaknesses. My suggestion? Keep praying for him. Keep inviting him to our gatherings.

Remember, our responsibility is to sow the seed. God reaps the harvest. Your job, my job, is to invite Dex and others to come into the fellowship of believers as we all seek a greater understanding of God's will and His way. Make sense?"

"Yeah, that's fair. He may surprise us all and return."

Juan appreciated Roberto's wisdom and understanding. It was different than what Juan expected, and the soundness of Roberto's approach nestled in Juan's spirit.

CHAPTER 9

A few Saturdays passed and the men's Bible Study continued strongly. One Saturday, at the end of class, after bidding fond farewell to several, The Chief caught up with Juan as he was getting in his car.

"Hey, Juan, how goes it?"

Juan stopped and greeted his instructor. "I'm good, Roberto. Real good. How are you?"

"Blessed and highly favored, my brother. Just wanted to check with you about your long-lost buddy."

"You mean, Dex?"

"Yeah, Dex. How is he?" asked Roberto.

"He's good. Like you predicted though, he has kinda pulled away a bit. Every now and again, I actually catch up to him and we talk. If we're talking about work or sports, he's cool, but if I talk to him about coming back to church, suddenly he has short notice appointments or some other excuse. But in his defense, as a plumber he can't always control when somebody calls him with leaking pipes."

"Yeah," Roberto answered, "but he isn't the only plumber in town either. We have plumbers at church who make main service, Bible Study, choir rehearsal, and all kinds of stuff." Roberto scrunched his face as he searched for encouraging words. "Encourage your friend to join us. Pray for him. Wait on God to move in his spirit. It'll all be resolved in God's due time."

Juan had heard similar in various sermons, studies and whatnot. It was a different case when it involved a friend, even if that friend had drifted away.

■

Meanwhile, Dex was still trying to hold it down in Frisky's on Saturday night. Drink specials and cover charge discounts added to a festive atmosphere. The music was loud and rhythmic as usual, but Dex didn't feel the same without Juan to watch his back, laugh at his efforts to pick up women, and be his wingman. None of his acquaintances were a true friend like Juan.

Dex was at the bar, watching clubgoers move around on the dance floor, when the bartender tried to catch his attention.

"Want another drink?" the bartender asked.

"Nah. I'm good." Dex shrugged, like he had the weight of the world on his shoulders. He seemed a bit out of place, the only guy looking glum in the party.

"You don't look like you're having fun tonight. I've seen you in here cuttin' up and acting a fool. Something about you doesn't look right. What's on your mind?"

"I'm good. Really I am."

"Okay. I take your word for it. But, if you really are, then you gotta buy something. Can't have you sitting at the bar without buying a drink. This *is* a business, ya know. "

Dex reached in his pocket, pulled out some bills and bought another beer. Something was tugging at him, something that wouldn't be cured by one beer or one dozen or one hundred. He was starting to wonder if this was all there was to life."

All these years of him thinking he was the life of the party. Frisky's was still up and running, people were still coming through the doors. Some of the people he tried hard to please and impress had moved on to different interests. Here he was, still playing the jester, still playing the buffoon for a changing batch of folks. This wasn't as enjoyable and substantial as he thought in other years. This perspective was sobering, since there was a consequence to the burning of time. For the first time in his life, he thought about his long-term existence. He thought that there was more to life than hanging out in a club. He also noticed the oldest persons there were probably not quite thirty years of age. He was twenty-seven. Did he want to spend another three years rummaging in his pocket for cash to buy another drink?

He decided enough was enough, left the club, and on his way home called Juan.

"You a'ite? What's going on, man?" Juan asked him.

"Man, I dunno." Dex paused and let out a little sigh. "I was sitting in Frisky's tonight."

"Your office, right?" Juan offered a sarcastic comment, which was rare.

Dex paused, as if to show his disapproval of his friend's feeble attempt at humor. "What I was gonna say was, I was sitting in Frisky's and something hit me. It wasn't as much fun as before. The same music was on, the same types of people were there, but something was different. It was like I was watching TV, watching people carry on but not being attached to the scene. You know what I mean, man?"

"Yeah. I hear you loud and clear. Maybe you're outgrowing the club scene."

"I don't know what it is, man. I've kinda felt this off and on for a few weeks now. I've been so used to going just to go. But, tonight, it all became clear. I don't want to be one of those old dudes chasing young girls, thinking I'm still cool and looking sad and worn out."

"You aren't the first person to get to this point. Won't be the last either. It looks like so much fun on TV or in a video. Real life, it isn't the only way to spend a night. There are other interesting things to do, grown-up stuff. You get to decide what."

"I can't believe you're giving up a chance to tell me what to do next. What's the matter with you, man?" Dex cracked himself up.

Juan paused. "Now that you see this for yourself, you can understand that the club can be a waste of time for some folk. What are you looking for there? We had this talk before, and your answer then was hangin' with the girlies.

Now, you start to see that there's a bigger world out there than Frisky's."

"You sound like my stepdad. Telling' me how to spend my time and what I'm missing out on." Dex wasn't angry, just mildly put off like someone who had heard the same advice from several people.

"Maybe your stepdad has been right all along. You're still young enough to do some things, different things. You don't want to be like some of these old dudes who ran in the streets until their expiration date came."

Dex thought about Juan's warning for a while. An awkward, prolonged silence stalled the conversation. He wondered what else had gotten into Juan as a result of his increased church attendance. Juan wasn't the same running buddy he was before.

CHAPTER 10

After a restful night's sleep, Darlene awoke refreshed. Soon, it was time to grab something quickly for breakfast, get dressed, and head out to work. She wasn't one for frequent daydreaming. She was very much grounded in the tangible, real world. But for a moment, she wondered what kind of relationship would be worth getting into. She had friendships and other relationships at church and at work. She hadn't thought much of romance over the last few years, and had gotten used to the freedom she derived from being single. Now, she thought that maybe she was actually missing something after all. She took just a few moments to allow herself to drop her guard and imagine that she had someone in her life. Oddly enough, it wasn't physical things she thought of.

It didn't matter in her reverie how tall he might be or how muscular, just a strong, fruitful, Christian man. She figured if he had that straight with God, all his other qualities ought to be representative. If nothing else, he should be able to hold a conversation. Sitting next to a man who couldn't put two or three sentences together to support a coherent thought would bore her.

The handful of times in her past where she actually took that chance proved more harmful than enjoyable. It was either the wrong guy or the timing was all wrong. Some fellas had the type of qualities that other ladies would love to have in a man. Some were bold while other men were well-versed in various social graces. Others were good-looking, by any standard. Funny thing, though. None of the possibilities were good for Darlene's spirit. Strange part was, she really couldn't put all the blame on the man, because if she admitted to herself, she wasn't always all in when meeting men.

She couldn't put her finger on exactly why she wasn't all that enthused when meeting men. Darlene was never the type of girl who got starry-eyed when a handsome man walked by. She hoped she would have enough Godly discernment to know when a man would or wouldn't be right for her. She never stopped to consider that one day perhaps God would allow a worthwhile man to enter her life. Question was, would she be ready?

Later that afternoon, as the weekly staff meeting started, Darlene found herself a little distracted for no real reason that she could put her finger on. A resource allocation question came up in her area of expertise. Normally, she couldn't wait to jump up and offer her opinion. This time, she barely opened her mouth.

After the staff meeting adjourned, Grant Kubiak, her division chief sidled up to her. Grant was once someone she thought could be the man for her. They'd known each other now for a few years. When they were undergrads in college, Darlene and Grant were close. In fact, they were so close that many of their friends assumed they would become a couple and live happily ever after. After all, she and Grant shared similar backgrounds and viewpoints on life. It was a bit of a surprise that they didn't hook up.

Darlene and Grant, who was several years older than Darlene, met in a Psychology class. At the time, he was a declared Psych major, while she needed the course as the usual freshman prerequisite class. On the seating chart, they were next to one another. First couple of classes, neither noticed the other. Like most freshmen, they had their heads down, taking notes and working hard at keeping up. Class three, though, Grant either found himself more relaxed, maybe hung-over, maybe a bit impulsive. He started popping off under his breath. Small remarks, nothing mean. Just stuff he found funny like the way the professor wore his comb-over. Darlene thought Grant was hilarious. Grant thought Darlene was beautiful.

Grant worked overtime trying to impress Darlene. It went from making her giggle in Psych class to walking her to the student union for lunch to study sessions in the campus library.

The summer before his junior year, Grant worked part-time for a local landscaping company. On one of his jobs, he met Helen. She had just graduated high school a few weeks before. In addition, she was making the beauty queen circuit throughout the region. That summer, she was "Miss Cranberry

Festival," "Miss Brisket," and first runner-up to another competition.

Grant became hopelessly smitten with Helen, and Darlene quickly became an afterthought. Their budding friendship slowed all the way down when he fell in love with Helen.

It was a whirlwind courtship with Grant and Helen getting married a year after they met. Then barely a year after they exchanged vows, Helen gave birth to a beautiful little girl they named Grace.

Grant and Helen were the perfect happy couple. Darlene was hurt that her and Grant's friendship took a huge hit, but she managed to shield it from family and friends. She went on with her life, and didn't see Grant again until she got the job at the newspaper where he happened to have worked for the past several years.

Darlene and Grant resumed their platonic friendship. He often confided in her, and much like college, he was still able to make Darlene laugh.

Things on the outside seemed perfect between Helen and Grant but behind closed doors things must have been entirely different because without any warning to Grant, one day Helen decided she'd had enough. Enough of Grant and enough of being a mother to their daughter, Grace.

Before Helen abandoned her family, she periodically hosted dinner parties for the people in Grant's division. Grace and Darlene hit it off immediately at one of those parties, and Grace claimed a role model in Darlene.

Now, with no woman in the home, Grant's home and personal life were in shambles. He had depended on Helen greatly when they were together. He overlooked her flirtations and her overt desire to be seen as beautiful by everyone who crossed her path. He overlooked that stuff until she actually left him for another man. Then, the things he overlooked in the past seemed like clues he ignored. Clues that his marriage was doomed. Since then, Grant threw himself into his work. He wasn't prepared to lose his wife. He certainly wasn't prepared to raise a daughter by himself. He didn't know how to cope, so he fell back to the only thing he knew well – work.

Grant wanted a different fate for his daughter, a different path than the one his wife had chosen. He saw in Darlene the type of woman he wanted his daughter to emulate.

Darlene could sense a level of neediness emanating from Grant, but she didn't want to bear the burden of his heartache and insecurity. She saw a ton of potential in Grace, but didn't know exactly how much to invest in the situation. She could hold up Grace, but felt someone else needed to roll in and help Grant.

Grant smiled a wan smile. "Hey, can we talk in my office for a minute? I won't take much of your time."

Darlene nodded, and the two of them walked to his office.

Grant's office was a small, windowless office halfway between two corridors. It had a partial vertical window on the door, so he could get an idea of who waited outside. The bookshelves and walls had pictures of him, Helen, and of course, Grace.

Grant coughed and offered Darlene a seat. She politely accepted.

"Darlene, I'm concerned about Grace. She's basically a good kid, but I would guess she's going through a lot these days, and I have no idea how to raise a pre-teen. I could use a little help."

Darlene prayed to God for the right words to encourage but not mislead this man in pain. "There are several ministries at the church I attend. I think it could be a big help to her. Also, there's a ministry for divorced folk too that might interest you."

Grant sat up a little straighter, leaned a bit more forward towards Darlene. "The divorce isn't final just yet," he retorted in a firm voice. "I hope Helen is going through a phase and just needs to see it for herself." Grant let the words trail off as if he was trying to convince himself through some internal logic that other folk weren't smart enough to understand.

Darlene cleared her throat and tried to offer words of encouragement. "My church has been a real support to me and others. God has done marvelous things in the lives of people there. If you want, I could take Grace with me some time."

"Sounds like a good idea. She likes you, she always has. If you don't mind, I'll have her call you, and you two can work out the details."

"That sounds like a great idea. I look forward to seeing her. It's been a minute."

Grant started to shuffle and rearrange papers on his desk. He stood up, signaling the end of their visit.

"Darlene. You've always been a good friend to me." Grant walked Darlene to the door. He tried to thank her, but felt himself get a little choked up. He stifled the emotion before it leaked out.

As Darlene left his office, Grant closed the door softly. He sank into his chair, closed his eyes, and tried his best not to let a single tear leak out from his eyes.

After the meeting with Grant, Darlene resumed a productive day. She knocked out some short-term tasks and requests for information, which left her feeling proficient and relieved. Taking a short break, she indulged herself in a moment of personal concern during the work hours. She prayed to God for guidance and wisdom in dealing with Grant. She felt that she knew enough about men to know that sometimes they would latch on to any port in a storm when things started falling apart.

Although she was no longer romantically attracted to Grant, in her past she found herself the target of unwanted affections when her attempt to be a gracious human was misread as her being attracted to this guy or that fella. In her spirit, she really wanted to help him in some tangible way, but not by becoming his inadvertent, accidental girlfriend. Also, she knew that Grace was at an age where she may become mouthy and headstrong. Darlene had seen similar cases at church, where young kids and teenagers came in surly and mean-spirited. Parents were at their wit's end, trying to figure out what to do.

It wasn't an absolute, though. For every child who came to Green Valley and joined the youth ministry, there was another one who participated fully but left years later with no spiritual growth. There were a few who left just as worldly and carnally driven as they were when they joined. Despite that, Darlene felt that Grace would benefit by being around young believers. Perhaps some of that direction would rub off on her. Perhaps the Word of God would help Grace grow.

Darlene could hear her spirit talk to the Lord. "Lord, I pray Your will be done in Grant's life and in the life of his daughter, Grace. You know what he's going through. His marriage is in trouble. His relationship with his daughter is at a crossroads. He doesn't know which way to turn, but I know he can turn to You, Lord. Thank you, Lord, for hearing my prayer." Darlene sat quietly for a moment and rejoiced, knowing that God would reveal Himself in Grant's and Grace's lives.

CHAPTER 11

Juan couldn't stop thinking about his conversation with Dex. His perspective scared him just a bit. He heard the words coming out of his mouth, counseling Dex in a tone normally used by older, smarter men. Juan wondered where that came from, since he recently wasn't that outspoken about how others should live their lives. It was just easier to let people live, let them carry on as they saw fit.

Juan thought back to the times in college when he was full of what he thought was good opinion and advice for all who crossed his path. Literally, he shot his mouth off at nearly every opportunity, thinking he was helping friend and acquaintance alike. But often, what started out as good advice became points of contention between him and those around him. A couple of potential friendships and one possible romantic relationship were directly damaged beyond repair because of what he thought was good advice, but turned out to be at the wrong time to the wrong person. After getting burned a few times, he learned to keep his mouth shut.

He wasn't worried about friendship in this case, though. Dex was impulsive and erratic on some things, but he was doggedly loyal. In his own way, he lived a consistent life when it came to his intent and his words. Like him or not, one always knew where one stood with

Dex. If Dex had an issue with something Juan said, he would blurt out his disagreement early on. That too threw Juan off, that Dex didn't immediately push back with a dissenting comment.

Maybe Juan's words had struck a nerve with Dex. He had, in his past, held grudges, cut some folk out of his life when he felt they didn't have his best interests at heart (but these days, who didn't act that way).

With all that, Juan couldn't rest. He had a stirring of excitement and trepidation in the depths of his spirit. He could feel it in his core, a different viewpoint than he held before. This time, it wasn't being outspoken for the sake of his own ego. It seemed different somehow. Maybe he was making way too much of it, but Juan let the thought creep through that maybe, just maybe he was growing up. Not just some young guy wandering through this life, but a fully-formed adult that had experience and sound judgment. *So this is what it means to let God lead my life*, he thought.

The phone rang. Juan sat up on his couch, reached for his cell, and answered with a groggy, "Hey, wassup man?"

"I got hooked up, man! Guy at work has two tickets to the ball game tonight. Looks to be standing room only, with the defending league champs in town. Our guys will probably get blown out, but at least we can see it up close. You in?" Dex asked.

Juan looked at the time on his cell phone. He had just enough time to get cleaned up and get to the arena. "Yeah, I'm in. I think I can make it."

"Cool, meet me at Will Call. I'll see ya in a few!" Dex hung up.

Juan jumped up off his couch and shuffled into his bedroom to get a quick shower and change of clothes.

In near record time, he was cleaned up and in his car. After twenty minutes on the interstate, Juan pulled into the west parking lot adjacent to the arena. He paid the attendant, found an empty parking space, and walked hurriedly to Will Call.

Dex was out front trying to chat up a lady in line. Her body language screamed *leave me alone*. Juan shook his head at the sight of the same ol' Dex. They walked to the concourse and soon were in their seats. The typical noises and activity around a ball game were evident. Music blaring. scantily-clad women dancing around in varying states of coordination and precision. drunken guys dressed up in garish costumes and face-paint.

Juan settled in to watch the game, which seemed like more of a social event than pure competition between evenly matched teams. Several local celebrities were spotted in courtside seats. Reporters from local network TV affiliates scurried about trying to score an interview between periods of game action.

Meanwhile, the match on the court was no

contest from the start. The defending champs went up early by a large margin. Soon, they doubled the score of the home team. The fans in attendance, sensing a blowout of epic proportions, rooted loudly for the champs. Those fans got their wish. The visiting team was like a tidal wave, enveloping the game and the hapless home team.

During the second half, Dex and Juan shot the breeze about various things, none of them serious.

"I gotta admit, Dex, I could never carry on like you did out in the lobby tonight." Juan took a gulp of his soft drink.

"Juan, it's attitude. That's all. Plus, sometimes I do it just to entertain myself. I guess I'm easily bored. I know that over the course of the day I'll meet several ladies, and odds are none of them will actually want me. I mean, look at me. I'm not all that good looking. not particularly well-built. For me to meet a girl, I gotta have some quality that sets me apart from you and every other brotha out there."

"Fake it 'til you make it, right?'" Juan wasn't actually buying this load of stuff from his friend, but once in a while he would egg Dex on to see what outrageous thing he would say next.

Dex, on the other hand, took their conversation with all the earnestness he could muster. "Man, it ain't fake when it comes to me. I'm dead-serious, straight-up with this. Although I have fun with it, I treat it serious."

"Serious fun, eh? In my opinion, you're working way too hard at this. Somewhere down the road, you gotta ease up. Save yourself some indigestion."

"To each his own, my brother," Dex responded. "To each his own." They slapped five, but Juan again found himself shaking his head and chuckling at his friend's perspective.

CHAPTER 12

Darlene's Wednesday at work had gone quiet and smooth, no big heartburn moments. She was even able to leave a bit early to pick up Grace. The day before, she volunteered to take Grace to church, and Grant was in complete support. So, after picking up her young charge, the two ladies rode to the church. Grace was subdued, even as Darlene tried to initiate conversation during the ride.

As they got out of the car, Darlene walked towards the part of the church where the youth gathered. Grace was normally a confident young girl, but the new surroundings coupled with unfamiliar faces left her a bit uneasy. She worked hard to not let it show, but her face clouded over with apprehension.

"Okay, kiddo. Here's the place where you'll hang out for the next ninety minutes or so. I'll come get you when we're done. I'll be right down the hall." Darlene pointed in the direction of the room where she would be.

"Bathrooms are off to the left. Sister Yolanda is in charge of girls your age. In fact, she's right over there," Darlene pointed in front of her. "I'll introduce you."

Yolanda Rincon was a heavyset lady in her early 60s. She was one of the original members of Green Valley. Despite burying two husbands and her youngest child, she always let God's light shine through her spirit.

"Sister Yolanda? Sister Yolanda? Do you have a minute?" Darlene walked over to where Yolanda was, with Grace in tow.

"Darlene, how have you been? Haven't talked to you in a while." Yolanda gave Darlene a big hug, then looked over Darlene's shoulder at the skinny girl. " Who is this pretty young lady?" Yolanda disengaged from Darlene and reached out to Grace. "Hello, I'm Yolanda. Who are you, and where are you from?"

"My name is Grace Kubiak."

"Well, Grace, I'm pleased to meet you. Since you're new here, stick close to me, at least until you meet some of the other kids. Walk this way, hon."

Darlene whispered to Grace, "See, I told you we would take care of you." She watched Grace walk towards the youth sanctuary. Darlene felt some measured relief in the appearance that Grace and Yolanda weren't mortal enemies from the start. Darlene watched Grace disappear around the corner of the corridor, then she turned towards the main sanctuary.

As she walked towards the sanctuary, she crossed paths with Juan.

Juan brought Dex with him that night, and Dex being Dex meant Dex had his head on a swivel, checking out every woman within visual range. Juan hissed a quick, "Put it away, man" as they opened each side of the double doors. Juan and Dex smiled at each lady who came in, including Darlene. Juan tried to make eye contact with Darlene, but she seemed to have other things on her mind. Dex, on the other

61

hand, was gooning it up, making goo-goo eyes at Darlene to catch her attention. Good thing she didn't notice his goofy behavior.

The service was inspiring. The pastor was out of town that week, so the assistant pastor preached from Genesis, first chapter, verses twenty-nine through thirty-one, about the power of seeds. He spoke eloquently about how all things have the seed of a beginning, but the beginning isn't certainly the end. He touched on how seeds have the good stuff inside to provide for the initial growth of the organism, much like how God plants His seed of Godly gifts inside each believer. He also reminded the gathered folks that God grants much freedom for each person to willingly serve him. The other side, though, is if someone chooses the path of disobedience, that person gets to live with the consequences of that disobedience, in essence, killing the potential of the seed inside.

After service, several small groups remained to fellowship, pray, and encourage one another. Dex was his usual self. He happened to see a female gather her book bag, and he hustled over to ostensibly help her. He really just wanted to try to chat her up. Juan waited at a distance, trying not to look impatient.

"Good evening. I'm Dexter Jones."

"I'm Sharon. Nice to meet you, Dexter. God bless you, and be careful out there." The woman broke contact.

Juan could see Dex was getting that *I'm gonna break through to her, even if it kills me* look on his face. Juan was compelled to step in to stop his friend from embarrassing himself.

"Sorry, but we gotta head out." Juan tried to rescue the young lady from the situation, but wasn't initially successful. Dex could be bulldog determined, especially when he wanted something.

"Leave? Nah man, we don't have to go just yet. But, if you gotta go, I can find a way home. Perhaps uh, Sharon, can give me a lift?" Dex was reaching deep into his back of verbal women-meeting tricks. This one failed like the previous one.

Sharon had a look of distaste on her face. She was just about to rebut Dex's suggestion when Juan spoke up.

"Nah, man. I'm the one who brought you, and I won't leave you hanging. Let's roll." Juan looked at Sharon and smiled slightly. "Take care, ma'am. See you around." He and Dex headed out of the sanctuary.

As they walked to the car, Dex couldn't stop jabbering. "Hey, man. Do you think I got through to Sharon? Do you think she'll be thinking about me later?"

Juan rolled his eyes just a bit. He wanted to play a sarcasm card, but couldn't. He was too busy thinking about the woman who he saw standing next to Sharon. Juan remembered that she was the same girl who he met when he first walked into Green Valley. He heard the person talking to her call her Darlene.

Juan had to admit to himself that Darlene was luminous. The way her hair framed her face was nearly perfect. She had a light in her eyes that any man would be drawn to. He was glad Dex noticed Sharon instead of Darlene. Darlene gave Juan something else to look forward to at church.

■

Grace came around the corner in the hallway and saw Darlene standing near the church's front door. Darlene looked over her left shoulder at the young girl and offered a reassuring glance. Grace showed a slight smile in return.

"You know, Miss Darlene, the kids were cool. If you don't mind, I'd like to come back with you next week. I exchanged a couple of numbers with some of the girls. Do you think my dad would mind me hanging out with some of the kids here?"

Darlene hadn't seen this kind of energy from Grace before. It wasn't Christmas or Grace's birthday, so most days she appeared to be like most young kids, distracted and uncooperative. Darlene felt a rush of encouragement seeing Grace's reaction. This fellowship might be just the thing the young girl Grace needed.

Grace hadn't hung out with many kids her age since her parents' separation. When her mom left her life, her parents' friends and their kids slowly faded away, too, leaving Grace torn. She loved her mom and desperately wanted her to return so they could be a family again, but, she also despised her mom for leaving her hanging in this sudden way. On top of that, Grace was left bewildered by her friends pulling away. Wasn't she the same Grace as before her mom's departure? Didn't she still like swimming and roller-skating, strawberry ice cream and high-top sneakers? She hadn't changed her style of dress or how she wore her hair.

Now, it appeared that Grace had found a place where she could actually fit, where people didn't judge her based on what her parents did. She could feel herself starting to feel better.

CHAPTER 13

Juan drove out of the church parking lot with the sound of Dex gushing about the girl, Sharon.

"Manoman, that female was something else. Whattaya think, man?"

Juan tried to play it cool. "Yeah, she seemed cool, but she didn't seem to have a lot of interest in your game, though. You can't approach girls like her in the same way you chase girls in the club, ya know."

"Dude, who do you think you're talking to? Who's the ladies' man here? Is it you? Naaah, afraid not. You and I both know I wrote the book on scooping up the girlies." Dex cracked himself up, like he often did. Juan just rolled his eyes again.

"All kidding aside, bro, I can see why guys flock to the church house. All kinds of talent walking around in there. I'm glad I came with you tonight. You got my back; I know that now more than ever. I think I'm gonna get involved in some of those ministries, make myself known."

Juan had heard enough. "Look, man. You and I both know you aren't serious. Being in God's house should mean more than trying to lay your mack lines down to the ladies. Plus you don't know if she's seeing another guy already. She may even be married. You've been in church before, you know what to do and not do."

Dex heard his friend's voice, but kept on babbling about how if she was seeing a guy or married, that the guy should have been with her. Dex also talked about how he had grown up in the church, a one-time powerful sentiment that had eroded over the years to a cliché about folk who walked through a church's doors only to walk out later with no real change to their spirits.

Juan felt more exasperated as Dex continued to jabber about what he was gonna do and the number of women he was going to meet.

As Dex kept talking, he could sense that Juan wasn't doing the verbal sparring they had done throughout their friendship. Dex stopped his discourse for a bit, and asked, "Wassup, man? Don't you have your usual correction and advice to offer?"

Juan thought for a minute. He really wanted to lash out at Dex, verbally goad him into submission and understanding. Something in his spirit slowed down his heart rate and growing frustration. "Man," he started, "I will offer this, on the church's website, are several Bible Studies and fellowships that are just for us men. You oughtta check one of those out, see if you like the teaching that goes forth and the fellas that show up. You may see things in a different light."

"Yeah, whatever." Dex said. For the remainder of the ride home, Dex was quiet for the first time all evening.

As they pulled up to Dex's apartment, the two exchanged a slap-five. Dex thanked Juan for driving. "I know the way there, bro. See you there sometime. Maybe not next Sunday–it depends on how late I'm at the club." Dex let out a sly laugh and sauntered to his apartment door.

■

Driving Grace home, Darlene was eager to find out more details from her about the youth session.

"Grace, I'm glad you enjoyed the fellowship tonight. Didn't I tell you that things would go well?" Darlene seemed truly encouraged and relieved.

"Yes, and you were right. The girls I sat next to were cool. I think coming back will be fun."

"Good, and remember, your dad can come as well. They have classes for men, too. What did you talk about in class?"

"We talked about purity. The minister had so many details, I couldn't keep up with it all. But, there were some notes passed around at the end."

"What do you think about the concept? I know it may be a bit much for you right now, but it may be the right time to start thinking about how you approach things, you know, like when boys come around trying to talk you into stuff." Darlene tried to be delicate, but like most girls, Grace tried hard to act older than she was.

"You don't have to worry about me, Miss Darlene. I know how goofy and slick boys can be."

Darlene smiled, but also remembered her assuredness from her own youth. *Young folk seem to have all the answers*, Darlene thought. *Haven't even lived a grown-up life yet. I hope she remembers her confidence tomorrow.* She refrained from giving the young girl the expected nagging warning, and went on asking about the rest of her experience.

Grace mentioned the substantial number of kids in attendance. She was relieved that the kids were outspoken and lively. She had heard all kinds of misinformation at school about how Christian kids weren't allowed to have fun. It appeared that Grace learned quite a bit on that night about God and about people.

As Darlene pulled up in the short driveway of Grace's house, she gave her car horn a short beep. A light came on near the front porch.

The front door opened and Grant appeared. "Hi, you two." He waved at Darlene and beckoned her and Grace towards the porch. "How was church?"

"It was fun." Grace looked over her shoulder at Darlene. "Can I go back with Miss Darlene next week,?"

"We'll see. In the meantime, you better go inside and make sure all of your homework's done."

"It is. Goodnight, Miss Darlene," Grace said.

"Goodnight, Grace."

Grant turned to face Darlene as Grace disappeared inside.

"I really appreciate you taking Grace with you tonight."

Darlene sensed Grant was having another one of those nights, pining for his long-gone wife. "You know, there are ministries and fellowships for men, and others for divorced and separated folks."

Grant grimaced. "You alluded to that before, but I think that would be a poor substitute for my wife coming back, don't you?"

"Moping about your situation is a poor substitute."

CHAPTER 14

Juan drove home slower than usual. As a guy who made a point of following every traffic law to the letter, and who all but demanded that others do the same while he was on the road, his lack of focus wasn't his typical way.

He found himself flashing back to times in high school and college. In school, he was one of those nondescript guys who was always around but less than memorable. Sure, he had a crush on this girl or that, but rarely did he actually date any of them. It always seemed the object of his desire was interested in some other guy.

When he was younger, it was easy to rationalize why girls didn't notice him. He would assume it was because he didn't have a car, or perhaps he wasn't a sports star or musician or even a drug dealer. He figured that since he wasn't in a high-profile clique or because he wasn't a notorious bad boy, then that must have been why the females appeared not to be interested.

One of the consistently irritating parts of high school life was the annual tradition of inviting a girl to prom, only to be turned down. By his junior year, different kids in his school took bets on just how vocal and shrill the rejection would be. Would the girl shriek like a banshee, or just walk away quietly when rejecting Juan. He would fret about it for days at a time.

When he started college, he realized that he wasn't the only one going through such rejection, and worrying about it wasn't helping him when it came to education and forging ahead with his dreams. So, during his sophomore year of college he pretty much gave up on romance and devoted most of his time to his studies. As far as compensating choices go, there were worse ones.

Sure, there were moments in the following years where loneliness crept up, but for the most part he threw himself into studying and performing community service. He was able to accomplish a high GPA, get what his peers considered a good job with a consulting firm, and he found time to mentor kids at a middle school near his college. His accomplishments made him feel some level of confidence, and kept him busy enough that he didn't lament his lack of romantic success.

Then there was Darlene. The sight of her stirred up feelings long dormant in his spirit. One of those feelings was the same old "here we go again" vibe. He had been down the path enough to where he automatically expected that she wasn't attracted to him. So, he fell back to his default position. *Don't bother her*, he thought. *She has something else going on, or some other guy in mind. Better to leave her alone than to get hurt.*

Despite his experiences and reluctance to get hurt yet again, Darlene had some kind of draw. He didn't discuss it with Dex. As much as he would like to write her off, something about the way she carried herself had him intrigued. His head told him not to get involved. His heart said something else.

CHAPTER 15

Darlene started taking Grace to Bible Study with her on a regular basis. Tonight was no different. After she bought Grace home, Darlene and Grant stood outside and talked. "Grant, I can see you're hurting – it's written all over your face.."

Grant's face clouded over, a sudden thunderstorm in full fury. He struggled for the right words. "These days, I don't know what to do." Grant was on the verge of unloading on Darlene, all the grief and rejection he had attempted to endure since his wife abandoned him and Grace. He had been trained by his dad to hold it in, never show weakness, never show pain. All that training was failing him now. He could feel tears burning his eyes. He looked over his shoulder. Grace was inside.

He tried to compose himself, then softly whispered, "Twelve years together and she just up and leaves. Guess I have to take that, but now the tough part is, our daughter is asking questions. Questions that make me think that she blames me for my her mother leaving. I don't know which is worse. The rejection from my wife, or the one person on this earth I have left to live for blaming me for my own hurt. Worst part is, I would take Helen back in a heartbeat. I don't even need her to apologize, just come back and act like she wants to be here with us, her family." Grant averted his eyes from Darlene, as if that could hide the tears.

Darlene sighed and shook her head sadly, commiserating with the man on the porch. "Grant, I'm not equipped to take away your pain, but I know God can and will. Turn your pain over to Him. Maybe Helen won't come back. Maybe no other woman comes around. But God is a consistent friend and support in good times and difficult times."

Grant heard his daughter's footfalls come near so he wiped his eyes with his sleeve. He was somewhat thankful it was dusk, maybe Grace wouldn't see he had been crying. He put his index finger to his lips, requesting silence from Darlene. Grace came into view, and poked her head around the doorsill.

"What is it, kiddo?"

"Can I stay up and watch a concert on TV? My homework is all done."

"Anybody I'm familiar with?"

"I dunno. I got the DVD from one of my friends at church. She said it's a Christian band, but they sound cool, like regular bands."

Grant had long been the disciplinarian in his family, but after Helen's departure, he found himself becoming more of a pushover for his daughter. "Okay, you can watch it. But if you find yourself starting to doze off, stop the DVD and finish it tomorrow. And you better not be dragging tomorrow morning when it's time to get up and get ready for school. Got me?"

"Yes, sir." Grace started to skip back into the house, then stopped. "Oh, Daddy, I forgot to tell you that the church is having a youth lock-in. It sounds like fun. Can I go?" Grace asked, looking up with pleading brown eyes at her dad.

Darlene couldn't help but giggle. Grant loved his daughter and rarely turned down her requests. Especially when the requests were for things that were for Grace's own good.

He looked at his daughter and responded, "Sure, when is it?"

"On the thirteenth."

"Okay, you got it, kiddo."

Grace pivoted on her heels and fairly skipped back into the house.

What a bubbly kid. So innocent and genuinely happy. Hopefully, life doesn't beat that out of her, Darlene thought.

Grant turned back to face Darlene. "I know you mean well, and really want to help. And, I'm grateful for you taking an interest in my daughter. But I gotta say I wonder about your suggestion for me. When I met Helen all of her acquaintances and friends said she was the most devout person they knew. All of them said that. It was one of the things I loved about her, her love for God. I knew I wasn't as far along as she was on faith, but I really thought we would grow together. We made a vow before God and man, and now she's dumped me. No warning no let me down easy or brace for impact, nothing. What kind of person who believes in God treats others that way?" Grant took a deep breath. He felt himself start to blush. He caught himself, took another deep breath and exhaled loudly. "I know you mean well, but I got too much hurt to wade through before I come to church."

Darlene waited a couple of beats, then searched for more words of encouragement. "None of us can get through heartache alone."

Grant stared at Darlene.

For a couple of seconds, Darlene silently prayed to God for more words to offer Grant, words that would help him get on the right track.

"You know, Grant, the lock-in can always use volunteers to provide informal security. That could be a place where you can help out. You don't have to answer now, but give it some thought." Darlene paused a bit. "You should get out more and do stuff. Not just any stuff, but stuff for others that takes you out of wrestling with your own problems. You've internalized way too much for way too long. Looking out after someone else from time to time may help you snap out of your funk."

"What do you think I've been doing all this time with Grace? I look out for her every moment of every day. So, you're telling me I'm supposed to put some stranger at the forefront of my life? Give time that I give to my flesh and blood to someone I haven't met? Sounds kinda goofy to me," he lashed out.

Darlene was taken aback by the sudden surge of anger from a man who just moments before was on the verge of tears. Mentally, she packed up any further advice she might have offered, generated a kind but distant tone and offered a curt, polite goodbye. She turned to walk back to her car. She couldn't help herself; she had to get in one last word. "I didn't mean to offend you. I just don't want to see you lose sight of what a wonderful gift life is."

"Gift, huh? Right now, I wouldn't mind giving back this gift. It hurts more than I would have ever expected." Grant also generated a kind and distant tone in his voice, echoing what he received from Darlene. "But, thanks again for taking Grace to church. Take care, see you soon." Grant wheeled around, opened the screen door, walked inside, and closed the door behind him.

Darlene was astute enough to know that Grant was on the verge of breaking. She could tell he wanted to reach out for some anchor that would keep him steady in the midst of this storm in his life. She also realized that like so many others, Grant had no idea where to seek help to get him through the next day. She knew God wanted to sustain him, but Grant appeared to want nothing to do with God right now. *Maybe tomorrow,* she thought.

She started her car, began to shift into reverse, and suddenly stopped. Instead of moving, she prayed again. She asked God to calm Grant's spirit and open his eyes to what was really going on around him. She knew that there was no profit in Grant fighting himself or staying in this season of frustration and grief.

CHAPTER 16

Normally, Juan got five to six disjointed hours of sleep each night. He had gotten used to living with some level of fatigue and sleep deprivation. However, last night, he slept seven hours straight through. He felt refreshed, more so than he had in months. He got out of bed, flexed his ankles, *yep, they still work*, and arose from his bed. He walked to his dresser to check his cell phone for messages. Nothing new, so he put it down and headed to the shower.

After he finished getting dressed, he headed out the door to work. The weather was unseasonably mild, so Juan got in his car and opened a window to feel a breeze as he drove along. He left the radio off, and enjoyed the feel of air rushing by his hand.

The commute went fast, and he found himself at work sooner than expected. As he pulled into the parking garage, he felt ready to take on whatever challenges the day brought.

Juan took the garage elevator to the fifth floor, strode down the hallway past allies and enemies alike, got to his cubicle, and logged on his work PC. He read the usual updates about going away luncheons, software upgrades to the network and the like. It appeared he could ease into the day and perhaps get some of his long-term projects completed.

When he started his career as an accountant, Juan quickly earned a reputation from his peers as being supremely focused. Nothing got in his way when he had a task in his sights. He possessed a bulldog tenacity, a trait his superiors really appreciated. They knew when Juan said a task was done, it was done and done well. Wasting time, like some of his coworkers who gathered around a water cooler like animals in the wild, held no allure for him.

Juan looked up from his reverie, reached for his mouse, opened up a couple of files on his PC, perused the info on the screen, and mentally shifted from personal thoughts to business issues.

Soon, the end of the work day had come with a sense of completion and satisfaction. Now that he was caught up, he felt a burning need for some outdoor quiet time, but it had started raining, so that was out of the question. Walking against the wind in the rain sounded ghastly. He didn't want to spend the evening holed up in his apartment. No movie at the local theater captivated his interest. None of his favorite local bands were playing that night. He normally didn't want to waste the money, but he gave it the old "what the heck" shrug and decided to drive around town a bit after work.

He shut down his work PC, grabbed his jacket off the coat hook in his cubicle, and headed to the elevator. Soon, he was in his car, driving out of the garage and onto city streets slick with rain, oil, and dust.

Light after light, intersection after intersection, it all seemed to blend in together as one mass of concrete, glass, and asphalt. Every building looked like the one he just passed. Every traffic signal cycled through the familiar green/yellow/red cadence in an almost hypnotic sequence.

At the corner of Oak Street and 17th Avenue, he found himself at his church. There was a banner outside the building advertising a speaker for that very night, in just a few minutes from the present time. Juan decided to pull into the parking lot and go hear what the speaker had to say.

Juan parked his car, searched for his umbrella in the back seat, and jogged toward the grand front doors of the church. He chuckled to himself noting the irony of a church named Green Valley in the midst of all this concrete and glass. The only green he could see for blocks in any direction was the green on the traffic lights.

As he walked inside the church, he was greeted by an enthusiastic usher who handed him a trifold program that described the night's topic and introduced the night's speaker. The usher pointed to his right and directed Juan to some open seats towards the middle of the sanctuary.

The sermon from Song of Solomon was spirited. The preacher was animated and the congregation readily joined in.

When the speaker finished, he prayed for the gathered congregation, that each individual would turn himself over to God's healing and direction in their lives. A brief benediction served as the close of the proceedings, and the gathered masses got up to leave the building, or just mill around a while.

As Juan got up to leave the sanctuary, he ran into Darlene. She looked stunning, dressed in business casual attire. He looked at her and started to speak, but Darlene beat him to it.

"How did you like the speaker?" she asked."

"She was smooth, real smooth. I especially liked the place where she talked about how committed God is in His relationship with us. It is continual and unbreakable, if I remember her correctly."

They made conversation as the both of them followed some of the other members upstairs to the coffee bar. The coffee bar was a quiet place where members could gather a bit after services and other programs. The selection of coffees and teas was extensive, and the member-volunteers were friendly and attentive. There were large windows that opened into the sanctuary so folks could sit and see the services while they finished their beverages.

After waiting in line a bit, Darlene and Juan ordered their beverages–chai tea for her, decaf with half-and-half for him. He settled the bill, and carried their drinks to an open table near a window overlooking the rain glistening streets below. He put the drinks on the table, pulled out a chair for Darlene, and took a seat opposite her.

Darlene took a taste of her chai tea then spoke. "To know that God loves us, well, that keeps me going day after day." Darlene's eyes sparkled as she recounted to Juan what she heard in the presentation and how God had revealed bits and pieces of similar information in her own life over the years.

Juan listened intently. Darlene's voice was warm and comforting. The more he listened to her, the more he realized she had a deep well of passion for God. She possessed a great command of language. The words she chose insured whoever conversed with her understood what she was talking about. Juan thought, *I could listen to her all day long*. He had gotten lax in his own conversational skills. Years of business-speak had locked him into a style of speech that was efficient in the work environment, but not useful when trying to connect with another human on a personal level.

The moments went by fast, and the couple lost track of time. Juan felt more at ease the longer he sat with Darlene. His own personality began to show more and more. Her body language denoted a similar ease with his company. As they found themselves further lost in the conversation, the Stephenson triplets sidled up to the table.

"Hey, Darlene. How you doing?" Candi spoke first. Cathi and Carli followed with hellos of their own. "Darlene, who is this gentleman?" Candi changed her gaze from Darlene to Juan. " Sir, we haven't met, but I am Candide Stephenson, and these are my sisters Catherine and Carlene."

"I'm Juan. Juan Smith." He stood and exchanged handshakes with each of the women. "It's good to meet you all. Can I offer to get you a cup of coffee or something?"

Cathi blurted out, "I'll have a mocha with whipped cream and caramel." Her sister stopped her with a wink and a nudge.

"No, thank you, but it's kind of you to offer," Candi said.

"Yeah, we gotta get home out of this rain. We saw Darlene and came over to say hi," added Carli, giving Darlene a knowing glance.

"Juan, what she meant to say is they saw me talking to you and wanted to come over and do recon." Darlene shook her head and fought hard not to crack up over the obvious snooping her friends were trying to accomplish.

"Darlene!" said Candi. "It's not recon. The word you're looking for is surveillance. Candi sounded stern, but the glint in her eyes betrayed the mischievous humor behind the remark.

Juan laughed a bit at the banter, even as he realized it was an inside joke that he wasn't privy to.

"Anyway, Juan, it was nice to meet you," said Cathi. "We look forward to seeing you around church."

"Are you involved with any ministries yet? Has God put you with some like-minded brothers here?" asked Candi.

"No, ma'am," he answered.

"I know the person in charge of home visitation and checking on the elderly who can no longer work their yards around their homes. They could use someone like you." Candi's leadership and forward-looking were evident. She could already envision four or five different ministries where Juan could serve. "I can put you in touch with—"

Carli stopped her sister. "Sis, we really should leave. Let these young folks have their meeting in peace."

Candi looked at her watch. "Yeah, you're right." Candi patted Darlene on the shoulder. "This lady is like the daughter I never had. I love her like my own flesh and blood." Candi kissed Darlene on the cheek. "Goodbye, young lady." She turned her gaze to Juan. "God bless you, young man. Drive safe out there."

Cathi and Carli echoed their sister's salutation and the three ladies started to leave.

Juan stood up. "It is getting dark outside. Can I walk you ladies to your cars?" He looked at Darlene. "You in? I can walk you to yours too."

Darlene agreed "Yeah, sure. Are we done here?"

Juan paused for a beat. "Maybe not done, but we can clean up, at least." He gathered up the now-empty cups, wiped the counter with a clean napkin, and threw everything away. After pushing the chairs under the table, he ushered the four ladies towards the door.

He enjoyed the casual conversation he heard the next few moments. Darlene and her friends were all in a buoyant mood, so the conversation flowed like good jazz. Each of the ladies had something pithy to add, and the laughter was free and easy. Juan could tell that the women were close and had an idea of how to relate to one another in a manner that was uplifting and worthwhile.

Soon, they were in the parking lot. The rain had subsided, and the Stephenson triplets got into their van with Candi at the wheel. She started the engine, gave the young couple a wave, put the van in gear, and peeled out of the parking lot with tires squealing.

Darlene and Juan looked at each other and shook their heads in laughter.

"Wow, those ladies are something else," Juan noted.

"Yes, they are." Darlene smiled at the thought of someone appreciating her friends. Darlene averted her eyes, then looked back at Juan. "Hey, it was good talking to you and hanging out a bit. I'm gonna head out now before this rain starts up again. But, I look forward to chatting with you again."

Juan brightened up. "Yeah, I had a good time." Juan started to say goodbye, but stopped. "Uh, how do I reach you in the meantime?"

Darlene reached in her purse and pulled out a business card.

Juan received it, looked it over, and saw that there was no phone number on it. Just name, job title, and work e-mail.

"Cool." Juan put the card in his wallet.

Darlene smiled sweetly and turned to walk towards her car with Juan escorting her. She unlocked her door, and he opened it for her.

"See you soon, Darlene. I had a great time."

"Me too, Juan. Catch you next time. God bless you, and be careful out here." They shook hands. He gently closed her car door.

Darlene started her engine and drove off.

Juan stood there for a moment in the church parking lot, soaking in the scene around him. The rain left the skies mostly obscured, but glimpses of stars were in various parts of the sky. For Juan, this was a night worth remembering.

■

Darlene got home and started off-loading all the stuff of the day. As she put her purse on her bed, she removed her cell phone to look for possible voice mail icons.

She felt light-hearted, an unfamiliar feeling. *He doesn't seem like a bad guy*, she thought. *But, most people put on a good first impression.* After she showered and then changed into pajamas, she reminded herself to not think in either extreme. She wouldn't see Juan as a possible date, but she wouldn't reject him either. Her spirit cautioned her to take things slow.

She chuckled a bit at the thought of her friends. They went out of their way to be nice to Juan. But Darlene knew they were really making mental notes about him. No doubt they would be ready to give her their impressions. Darlene need only ask, and they would flood her with their observations.

She had to get a grip. It was only one meeting, only a few minutes. Darlene turned down the covers on her bed, took to her knees, and began to pray.

She finished, got to her feet, turned off the bedroom light, and slid under the covers. *He's probably not giving any thought to me other than some girl he met at church.*

CHAPTER 17

"Juan, my brother, wassup?" Juan shook his head. Where did Dex get all this energy? Juan, at that moment, realized he shouldn't have even answered the phone. That's why voicemail existed, after all.

"I gotta tell you, man. I didn't go to Frisky's tonight. Instead, I went to a book club. Manoman, the quality of ladies there was some kinda impressive, I'll tell you."

"Dex, I gotta admit, I *am* impressed. You appear to be branching out in your social adventures. What are the guys at Frisky's gonna do when they see you carrying around a book bag?" Juan possessed a sense of humor, but it seemed only he laughed at his attempts.

A slight pause, then Juan continued. "I met someone myself at church tonight. We didn't talk a lot, just shot the breeze for a bit. She seems smart, real smart. Can't say that I know her enough to say I gotta pursue, but she seems like cool people. Guess it remains to be seen how she reacts next time I see her."

"Does she have a twin sister?"

"C'mon, man.

Dex started laughing over the phone. "Remember the last time you talked like that? What was it, high school, that time you talked about that cheerleader we met at a homecoming party? First time you talked to her she seemed so sweet and interested. Next time we saw her, she wouldn't speak to you and accused me of being a stalker."

"That's because you *were* stalking her, and she blamed me for it. Dunno why she was under the impression that I put you up to it. You thought it was funny, but it took weeks for that to get resolved."

"Juan, you gotta admit her transferring to another state that summer helped you out big-time."

"Man, what a relief. Why did her family move again?"

"I heard that her dad was an informant for the FBI. Used to be a bookkeeper for the mob or some such. They had to move when they went into the Witness Protection Program. Things got a little hairy. Bad guys were looking for her dad; they had to book out of town 'on the hop'. Wow, what a life. If that was me, I don't know if I would want to give up all the good deals and stuff I've built here. So many people would miss me. What would they do with no Dex in their lives?"

Juan always wondered when Dex went down that road of narcissism, how much of it was legit and how much was put-on.

Juan took a breath. "I know this is good stuff for you to chew on, but I got an early day at the office tomorrow. Can we finish this later, like next time we hit the gym?"

"Yeah, but keep me posted about her. I'm serious about whether she has a twin. If she is prospect enough for you to be interested, then there has to be at least one more like her somewhere nearby. You know how women are, how they hang in packs. Know what I mean?"

"Naw, all I know is any type is your type. But, anyway, I'll keep you posted. Be warned, she isn't like the chicks you meet in the streets. Her conversation may be too deep and mature for you."

"Bro, I have different words for different ladies, because I'm just that type of quick-on-my-feet type of cat that can keep up with the smartest of ladies. Verbal agility is what it's called. But, yeah, it's time for me to scoot. Catch ya later."

"Yeah, later." As Juan hung up, he let himself daydream just a bit. What if there was a chance for something serious to develop between him and Darlene? What if she wanted to be more than a casual acquaintance? Juan was intrigued, maybe more than just intrigued. Something about Darlene struck him in a new place.

CHAPTER 18

Thursday normally was Juan's favorite day of the work week. His boss and the counterpart leaders tried to build a weekly team-building exercise into the schedule most weeks, workload permitting. One week, a group trip to a laser tag-type place was on the schedule, while another Thursday meant a trip to an aviation museum to get insight on how teamwork enabled folks to push the envelopes of engineering and flight. The bosses put some effort in making their team-building days something that tied into better working relationships in the office. They usually didn't find out what the team building exercise involved until they arrived on the particular Thursday, so there was some suspense and anticipation as they reported to work.

There was just enough time for each employee to come in, check e-mail and voice mail messages for urgent tasks, grab a coffee to go, then head back to the garage to get in a rental courtesy van for a team-building trip.

Juan took a peek at his e-mail–nothing there of importance. A cursory voice mail check disclosed the usual messages from other departments and outside messages from professional organizations with various requests. *This stuff can wait until tomorrow.* He fleetingly wondered if, perhaps, Darlene had ferreted out his contact info. With all sorts of investigative means available, he didn't have to force his phone number on her last night for her to dig it out. Maybe that initiative would show her interest, make it easy for him to determine if she was worth his time.

Just as he thought that, he realized that any woman who carried herself with a sense of grace and poise wouldn't chase after some guy she had only conversed with once. Darlene was that lady of grace and poise, if nothing else. Juan couldn't help but laugh at himself for being so self-centered.

He logged off his work computer, gathered a small pack of bubble gum from his desk, and headed towards the elevator. Whatever this play day held, it would be a nice change of pace from the normal grind.

Meanwhile, across town, Darlene arrived at her office earlier than usual. The rain from the day before had been replaced by a beautiful, crisp, clear day.

A couple of local firms had recently laid off scores of employees, putting a dent in the city's economy and putting other companies in town on notice. If the economy continued to sputter, other services and products would see a decline as well. Darlene was tasked to write a column that captured the mood of the city, while at the same time noting the potential growth opportunities that could provide a short-term economic uplift. This was the toughest part of her job–trying to capture issues with her voice, not being swayed by bosses or influence peddlers, while at the same time not being too consistently pessimistic nor unrealistically optimistic. Regardless of what forces were at play, she was struggling to put her thoughts on paper.

As she started typing out her column, she realized the initial draft was a fairly bloodless series of syllables. She had to do something to break out of her slump. Anything less would be a disservice to her readers.

As the time approached nine o'clock, Darlene figured a break would be worthwhile. She decided to go to the courtyard area with a cup of tea, thinking the sounds of chirping birds would help her get that sense of clarity she struggled to find up to that point.

She went downstairs to the ground floor snack bar, purchased a hot chai tea, and went outside to the adjacent courtyard. It was a beautiful morning, and she could feel herself start to relax. Her good mood lasted approximately seventy-five seconds.

Two younger ladies came outside to gossip, loudly. Darlene tried to keep her emotion at bay, but found herself a bit put off. She didn't recognize them; they must have been from a different floor of the building. They were giddy and loud like folks who wanted surrounding people to hear their intimate business. These two were gushing about a guy they saw the night before in a local gym. One young woman couldn't help herself, talking about how fine the guy was. The other lady fairly swooned over his deep, resonant voice and his hazel eyes. Darlene couldn't help but shake her head in what appeared to be two shallow young ladies, celebrating what in actuality were some of the more surface qualities a man might possess. The thought ushered Darlene into a bit of reminiscing.

Since the disastrous turn of events with Grant all those years ago, Darlene had never experienced a long-term relationship in the classic sense. There was one guy, a while ago, who showed an interest. His name was Michael Scott. To Darlene, Michael, in no level of exaggeration, was one of the most handsome guys she'd ever seen. He was six-five, probably two hundred pounds, with slate grey eyes, thick wavy hair, a dry sense of humor and a level of personal magnetism. Women loved him while men seemed to hold on to their girlfriends a little tighter when he walked by.

It was at a banquet downtown for local media members, that Darlene and Michael crossed paths. As with everyone, he made a dazzling first impression with her. Despite her normal reluctance, she took a chance on Michael. Within days, she learned the deeper meaning of regret.

It didn't take Darlene long to figure out that Michael wasn't right for her. He didn't have a relationship with God, and he carried himself like God couldn't do anything for him. Darlene didn't have any trepidation or remorse when she cut him loose about a week after meeting him.

Since then, Darlene made a point of avoiding guys like Michael, guys who took too much care of their public image. If a guy was too handsome, too poised, or too engaging, she would shut down and not let herself get drawn in. To the outside world, it was no big thing. No one ever seemed heartbroken about her choice.

This flashback led her to wonder about Juan. He wasn't impossibly good-looking, but he wasn't hideous either. In the short time they talked, he didn't seem overly self-aware or self-possessed. In a lot of ways, he seemed like a normal, average guy, and it appeared he was seeking God to lead his life. Maybe, just maybe, it was time for her to consider having someone to share her life. Darlene wondered how this would go over with Juan. She didn't want to appear forward or desperate, but she did want him to know that she wouldn't be against the two of them getting to know each other better. If it only went as far as platonic friends, that would be cool, too. If it became something more, then Juan would have to prove he was up to the challenge.

CHAPTER 19

Juan couldn't hide his bewilderment at the turn of events. The team building event was supposed to be a stress reliever. Instead, it produced four sprained ankles, a broken finger, and a swollen eye. Juan was happy to be home after such a fiasco.

"Man, your people are scary dangerous. How many folk get hurt playing ultimate Frisbee, especially the injuries you described. Were y'all playing a tackle version? Just clumsy? What was it?" Dex couldn't help but laugh. "I don't mean any harm, but you and I both know it does sound a little goofy."

"Embarrassing is what it is. I mean, who dives for a Frisbee? We're not kids any more. I doubt we do anymore team-building exercises in the next few weeks. Out with the field trips, in with the seminars. I can see it now. Eight hours of talking and viewing charts, eating stale donuts, and drinking lukewarm coffee. We won't learn anything, but at least we'll be out of our cubicles."

"Your co-workers must really be a bunch that didn't play much in school. Maybe next time y'all will play something simple, like hopscotch or foursquare. You can work your way up to dodge ball or something."

"Alright, alright. Dex, I get it. You think it's funny. Nothing but a nuisance to me." Juan was getting mildly perturbed just thinking about how goofy the outing ended up. All he wanted to do was an honest day's work and then go home when that work was done. He wasn't much for all the after-hours socializing. Changing the subject, Dex inquired, "What about that female you met at church? What's her name?"

"Darlene."

"Darlene. Pretty name. You should take a chance and get to know her. Ladies like her don't stay free forever. Some guy is gonna come along and work at it, really pursue her. Eventually, she'll cave. You, on the other hand, will sit back being cool, and, one day down the road, you'll regret not making that move. I bet she would enjoy you reaching out to her. In fact, she may be waiting for your call at this moment. It don't take much, man. Not much at all."

"Yeah, I guess so."

Darlene was graceful and kind. She could hold a conversation, and actually acted like she wanted to listen to his pronouncements. That, to Juan, was a lost skill in the present-day.

"I better let you go. Take it easy, bro. See ya at the gym Saturday, right?"

"Yeah, I need some time in the gym."

"You bet, bro. Call that woman, man."

"Yeah, yeah. I hear ya. Later."

"Later, bro."

CHAPTER 20

Darlene completed her column late Thursday evening. She came in early Friday morning to give it the once-over. After a few swift edits, she felt fairly satisfied with her efforts. She forwarded the draft to the editing department, and went back to scouring the local independent papers and other open source documents for ideas to use in upcoming columns.

As she did some informal study, her manager came by. "Darlene," he stated in a rich baritone voice. "I was in the Editing department when your column came in. I took a peek and loved what I saw. Loved it. I know you were here late last night. I also know you rarely, if ever, take time off. Tell you what, why don't you take the rest of the day off. Get out of here. That is a direct order, young lady."

Darlene made a minimal effort to protest, but it was wasted effort. Since she realized she wouldn't win the discussion, she commenced with logging off the computer and gathered her things so she could head out of her office. As she packed up for the week, she said a quick prayer. "Thank you, Lord, for the opportunity to touch lives."

Once she got outside, Darlene took several deep breaths of fresh air. It was good to be off work early. Traffic wasn't as hectic as usual, so driving home would be simple and pretty much stress-free.

As she started her engine and headed out of the parking lot into traffic, Darlene happened to see Juan driving by. He was heading south, and seemed to be relaxed behind the wheel. Since she was off work and had free time, impulsively she decided to follow him for a bit just for fun. It was the type of thing she normally didn't do. She made a point of not being directly behind him, tailing him like detectives she'd seen on television time and again.

She followed him at a distance for several blocks until he turned into the parking garage of Lanier, Mitchell and Northside, a prestigious accounting firm. She thought he must be in the midst of a promising career. She had known folks who worked there in other years, and garage parking was at a premium. Most rank-and-file employees there parked outside. Maybe Juan was worth knowing after all. A car alone or position in a company alone wasn't enough. Based on his position, though, perhaps he was the type of guy who could be thorough in other aspects of his life.

CHAPTER 21

Juan's week was grinding slowly to an end. He decided to e-mail Darlene. He did and included his office phone number. Within a few moments, she called.

"Hey, I'm glad you called. I've been thinking about you. How is your day going so far?"

"It's going well, thanks for asking. My boss gave me half-a-day off, so I'm cruising around the city before going home. I saw you a bit ago driving south and pulling in at the LMN Building. How long have you been working at Lanier, Mitchell and Northside?"

"A couple of years or so. Hey, you were following me? You some kind of detective or something?" Juan chuckled softly.

"Well, now that you mention it, I have had some experience on the streets and I have watched some detective shows and movies. I have a keen sense of tracking and discerning clues. I don't know what got into me. I guess I was feeling a little goofy."

"Pretty impressive, Darlene. Impressive and a bit scary. I never noticed you behind me, and I usually do a pretty good job of being aware of my surroundings. Yeah, pretty impressive indeed. What else do you know?"

"Well, I know lyrics to a few doo-wop songs. I know how to grill, and I know a great coffee place near where we both work."

"I admit, doo wop isn't my strong suit. I, too, know how to grill. I'm not much of a coffee drinker, but I could be coerced into spending time with a detective. Maybe learn a few techniques."

"Given that I brought up coffee, don't feel you have to buy. We can go Dutch, or I can buy. I have one of those membership cards at this place and the more I buy, the more I save. Yay, me."

"Well, the least I can do is help you save. Tell you what, you pick the time, and I'll be glad to treat."

Darlene paused for a beat, two beats, three beats. "How about now?"

"I can be there in twenty minutes. Is that 'now' enough for you?"

"Yeah, that'll work. See ya shortly," Darlene said before ending the call.

Twenty minutes later Juan walked into the coffee shop. Darlene was sitting near a window, her auburn hair shining with a rich warm tone in the midday light. She was completely gorgeous, pretty enough to take his breath away. As she saw him approach, she let a small smile escape her lips, and ran her right hand through her hair from front to back.

"Darlene, it's good to see you. You look great. Is early release your secret? You know, for staying youthful and dewy-fresh."

"I don't know anything about dewy-fresh. You gotta quit watching those infomercials." They both giggled at her humor.

Juan sat for a moment, searching for something to talk about. "So, what's the deal about grilling?"

"I have relatives in San Antonio. Spent many summers there. From an early age I learned several things about cooking outside. One, you gotta have plenty of dry wood. Two, you gotta have the time to cook the meat slowly; slow cooking makes all the difference. Next, spices and marinades have to be used sparingly, just enough to excite the taste buds, not so much to have the spices overcooked. Oh, yeah, one more thing. You gotta have a shady spot. Grilling in the brilliant sunshine in the dead of summer isn't wise."

"Sounds like you've stood over a grill once or twice."

"You betcha, and have always enjoyed doing it. Half the fun of grilling is hanging out with friends or family talking smack about who's the better cook, who has the better marinade plan, how long you leave meat on the rack before you turn it over, stuff like that. How about you? What about your grilling experiences?"

"My family is mostly in Tennessee and a few in Mississippi. Grilled lots of pork, chicken, hot dogs, hot links, you name it. Mine was similar to yours. Get up early, get the fire going. Cook the meat slow. Keep the fire going all day, folks working in shifts. Cook lots of meat so everyone gets to take some home. Boy, those were some good times that went by all too quick. Most of the ones I learned from have passed on, but the memories are good ones, though. You know, we ought to get together sometime, compare grill techniques."

"That would be good. What do you do in your spare time?"

"Well, the assumption is I have a lot of spare time. I spend a lot of time at work. I'm a CPA, and I really enjoy what I do. Probably enjoy it too much, since I spend a lot of time at the office. My friend, Dex and I work out at the gym on most Saturdays."

"Is he the fellow you brought to church? The one hitting on the ladies?" Darlene asked.

"Yes, that's Dex. Been best friends since kindergarten. And yep, he forever thinks he's the ladies man."

Juan wanted so badly to tell Darlene how beautiful he thought she was, but he sputtered the start of that statement.

"I guess Dex knows a lot of girls, huh?"

"Only in his head. Let him tell it, he's in constant demand."

"What about you?"

"What about me what?" said Juan.

"Do you know lots of girls?"

"I've met a few over the years. Things just didn't last for various reasons. None are enemies, though. If I see any of them on the street or in a mall, we normally can be cordial and civil. Most have moved on to marry other guys. One moved out of state, California I think. One joined the CIA, moved to the DC area as some kind of intel analyst."

"Wow, sounds like you've known some successful women."

"I guess. All in what you consider successful." Another awkward pause. Juan cleared his throat. "How about you? I'm sure there are guys who are waiting for you to notice them, what with your obvious beauty and all."

Darlene fought the urge to blush, but she lost that fight. "There may be guys waiting, but they're waiting in vain. Every once in a while, some guy approaches but his approach is all wrong. If he has nothing worthwhile to say, I lose interest quickly." Darlene caught herself and hoped she hadn't turned him off by providing more info than he was ready to absorb.

"Hey, do you realize we've been sitting here for half an hour but haven't ordered anything? What would you like? I'll go get it."

"Chai tea, please. Thank you."

"Okay, be right back."

Darlene watched Juan walk across the room to order their beverages. She was an astute observer of body language, and sensed Juan was poised and maybe a bit closed off. He could stand to loosen up a bit.

Meanwhile, Juan couldn't help but notice that while Darlene was obviously confident and talented, he suspected there was a bit of insecurity deep inside. Maybe that insecurity drove her to help others. In the previous time their paths crossed, he noticed she gave off a strong desire to obediently walk in God's

106

service. He thought that was an admirable quality, and it made her even more attractive in his eyes.

The order was complete. Chai for the lady and a double espresso for him.

"A double? Wow, Juan. I'm impressed, or should I be worried?" Darlene laughed. "Do you need that kind of rush this time of day?"

"Nah, nothing to worry about." Juan took a gulp of his drink. "Tell me more about Green Valley. How long have you been there? What led you there?"

Darlene glanced up for a moment, gathering her recollections. "Let's see. I've been a member for about six months. A co-worker recommended it. I visited, absolutely loved it, and then prayed about it for several days, asking God to make it evident if I was supposed to be there or not. And of course, like He always does, God made it evident."

"What happened that convinced you?"

"God revealed some things that I hadn't told anyone, things that came to pass, and that's when I knew in my spirit that Green Valley was the place. Since then, things have been enlightening and stable."

"I never thought about actively asking God to plant me in a specific church. I went with my folks as a kid because that was where they went. As an adult, I sought out churches that were similar. And boy did I. They were similar all the way down to the problems. Trustees embezzling funds. Members putting their own desires before God's direction. Members only coming to service when they felt like it, or leaving early if the pastor preached against something they didn't want to confront."

"Yeah, sounds like worldwide phenomena."

"You know it. That was a real eye-opener for me. I had to pretty much re-learn what to look for in a good church. Flash-and-dash took a back seat to real Biblical study. I don't mind admitting that Green Valley has been a relief. It seems like the pastor is squared away with the Bible. The few folk I met there seem stable in God. Not a whole lot of chasing worldly trends. I think I can stay a while, get to pitching in around there on some level, at least as my workload allows. You know how the office can be; sometimes your time isn't your own."

"Yeah, I hear ya. In some ways, when I was a younger reporter, my schedule was more directed down to me, but it only took a certain amount of time to research and write a story. Now, as a columnist, the time requirement is more fluid. I can get to a Bible Study in addition to the sermons on Sunday."

Darlene found herself a little more at ease talking to Juan. Not like he was a long-lost friend, but at least as someone who could hold a reasonable conversation. It felt good, better than she had experienced in a long time. She could feel her emotional barriers dropping.

Hours passed quickly, and before Juan and Darlene knew it, the sun had started its descent below the horizon. Neither wanted their getting acquainted time to end. Each had gone through multiple refills of their respective beverages, with Juan eventually switching to ice water. He could only stomach so many espressos.

"Darlene, as much as I've enjoyed this, I probably ought to head home. Gotta full schedule tomorrow, but I definitely would like to see you again, though."

"I'd like that," Darlene responded.

The couple confirmed each other's phone numbers in their respective cell phones. Juan made a point of taking a mental picture, associating the number with the luminous face across the table from him. He let a little smile slip from his lips.

As the couple got up from the table, Juan gave the table a quick wipe with a couple of napkins. Darlene noted that Juan seemed to possess a sense of neatness about him, from the act of cleaning up behind himself to his attire.

Juan noticed as they got up that Darlene was a graceful lady. Her posture was impeccable, and though her figure was more athletic she was still womanly. He let himself imagine the two of them being dressed up and on a formal date. He could envision her looking radiant and classy. He felt he would not be disappointed whenever he took her out.

Darlene tried to catch herself and not seem too terribly anxious. She wanted to socialize with Juan again. She wondered, however, about his relationship with God. All this discussion and he hadn't mentioned anything about God's influence in his life. She had seen him at church, but a lot of insincere folk walked through church doors. Her attraction was tempered by a real concern that they might not be compatible spiritually.

Juan sensed her being a bit wary, but he didn't know exactly why. "Not to pry, but it shows on your face that something is on your mind. Is there something you want to say?"

"Actually, there is."

"Let it rip, then," Juan urged.

"Well, I've noticed you at church, obviously. I want to know if you're really into it. Is your spirit growing under God's influence?"

Juan thought about it for a moment. "Well, I do realize that God's grace has kept me going. I also realize that I can hear and learn more about His purpose by coming to church."

Darlene wanted to ask more, get greater depth of understanding regarding Juan's walk with Christ, but she didn't want to ask him every question about his spiritual walk on their first meeting. She filed away her concern with the intent to ask later. She let out a shy smile.

"So, when is a good time to call you?" Juan asked.

"You can call at almost any time. However, normally around eleven o'clock I pray a bit and go to sleep, so I purposely don't answer the phone.

"Well, I tend to stay up late, so you can call me any time."

110

"Sure." Darlene looked at her watch. "I'm gonna head out now. Maybe we could do coffee again, or a movie or something." Darlene let it trail off, hoping Juan would fill in the blank with some interesting idea that a young couple could enjoy together.

"Sounds good. I don't get out nearly enough. Hanging out with you and learning more about the city could be a great combination. There has to be some museum to visit or hiking trail to experience. I'll come up with some ideas, and we can choose something." Juan walked to the coffee shop door, opened it for Darlene, and followed her to her car. He felt this could be the start of something good.

As she walked to her car, Darlene thought Juan had potential. Hanging out with him could be pleasant, with some minor tweaks to his habits.

Darlene's drive home was uneventful. She got inside, put down her small leather purse on the bed, and started to change clothes. The day had been interesting, and she was glad to get home and relax a bit. She got out her Bible and read a few scriptures.

Next, she started preparing dinner. She was in the mood for something light, as well as something she wouldn't mind having the next day as leftovers. A salad and some pasta with a light marinara sauce sounded tasty.

As she gathered her ingredients and started to boil water, she thought about Juan again.

He seemed to be a man still growing into himself. Did she have the time and the desire to walk beside him as he worked through his growth? Spiritually, he seemed somewhat blasé. The lack of spiritual grit in his demeanor gave her cause for pause. In her walk with Christ, she had seen others come from a further point off-course to get right with Christ. She felt that Juan wasn't that far off.

Darlene heard the pot of water beginning to boil. She opened the package, slowly poured the contents into the water, set the stove timer for eleven minutes, then went over to the kitchen table. As she took her seat, something came over her spirit. *This is a good time to pray.* "Heavenly Father, I praise you for being the one, true God. I ask your forgiveness for my sins and pray your continued guidance in my life. Lord, you see how I have crossed paths with Juan. I don't know what the future holds for us, but whatever happens between us, I pray that you are smack-dab in the middle of it. Regardless of what happens between me and Juan, stir up a fire in his soul to get closer to you. I love you, praise you, and exalt you above all others."

◼

Darlene had dinner, cleaned the kitchen, and readied for bed. She read a chapter of the book of James. She felt at peace, knowing that as long as she was obedient to God and took the time to listen to his advice, she would be where she needed to be.

She hit the carpeted floor and started some mild stretching. If nothing else, she was consistent. Since her time playing tennis in high school, she made a point of stretching every single night before bed. Taking her time, monitoring her breathing as she exerted, she could feel the cares of the day fade away. She was nearly complete when her cell phone rang.

"Hey, it's Juan. Just checking in with you. I had a good time with you today."

"Thank you, I enjoyed it too." Darlene noticed her reflection in the mirror, as she unconsciously smoothed her hair as if Juan could see what she looked like at that moment. She stopped once she noticed herself. "What's going on in your world this evening?" she asked him.

"I decided to hit the gym after I left you, went to a spin class. It was challenging but good."

"Good for you. How long have you been doing it?"

"Off and on for a year now. Used to ride when I was in college, mostly trails. One day last year, I found I missed doing it but the weather that day was pretty foul. I went to the gym that day after work, saw a co-worker heading into a spin class, poked my head in the room and thought it looked cool. The next day, I brought my gear and joined in." Juan chuckled. "I thought it would be easy, after all I consider myself to be in pretty good shape. That class kicked my butt and from then on, I was hooked." He laughed again. "How about you? What's your workout regimen like?"

"At work we have a pretty decent workout room. I don't use it nearly enough. I guess I'm blessed with decent metabolism. That, coupled with diligent tracking of what I eat, and I usually don't struggle with weight. I'm a tennis buff so I play whenever I have some free time. I also stretch a lot to maintain flexibility. I could stand to go back to running, riding, elliptical or something."

"Cool." Juan completely blanked on what to say next, resulting in an awkward pause. "I, uh, just called to tell you to have a good night. I'll call you tomorrow sometime. Perhaps we can figure out where we can go next time."

"Oh, you that sure that we're going out again?" Darlene offered her response as a little tweak, a shot at humor.

"Aw, sure. I suspect that hanging out with you will be a blast. I also guarantee you'll have a good time."

"Alright, then. I'm going to take you up on that. I'll let you make the plans and surprise me. But, and this is a small but, if I don't have a good time, what does your guarantee get me?"

Juan held off before answering. "If nothing else, I guarantee trying again, obviously by doing something different than what didn't work the first time." He held off another beat or two, waiting for Darlene's reaction.

"Good answer." She couldn't hold back her giggle, though.

Juan felt a sense of relief. *She seems like she's game, for a reasonable choice. And she has a sense of humor. This should work.*

"So, I guess I'll turn in."

"Pleasant dreams, Darlene. Talk to ya tomorrow."

"Goodnight, talk to ya tomorrow, Juan. God bless."

"Goodnight, and God bless you, too."

CHAPTER 22

The following morning Darlene got up and went about doing her normal morning regime of devotion time, reading a few scriptures and some stretching. She felt that familiar peace she recognized in her spirit as being from God.

As she got up from the floor to go start the coffee maker, she allowed a thought or two about Juan to cross her mind. Conversely, she did have some concerns about him. The logical Darlene thought, *Keep your distance. Let him demonstrate his thirst for Christ.* The emotional Darlene, the Darlene she kept locked away deep inside, saw the potential inside him versus the actual, on-the-street version that was obvious.

She realized that God had everything under control, and that she didn't have to worry about Juan's walk with the Lord. She also realized she had given Juan much more thought than she normally gave to a man. She usually kept her cool when men approached her to the point where most men thought she was anti-social or aloof and unreachable. The rare man who took the time to dig deeper found her to be a fascinating conversationalist, a loyal friend and the possessor of a biting wit.

All in all, the men who took the time to really listen to her ended up liking her. Unfortunately, she usually didn't feel the same towards them. After all, even with her warm and giving personality, she had her limits. She felt life was too short to waste moments with men who weren't squared away spiritually and didn't have the staying power to carry on with a woman who truly and literally put God at the forefront of her life.

■

Juan got to the workplace without getting too angry at the drivers around him. The usual tailgaters, fast lane blockers, and cell phone weavers that normally upset him didn't get to him on this day. In fact, he barely remembered driving to work because Darlene was on his mind that much.

"Juan," his boss spoke with a rumbling voice. "Get on my calendar before the week is out. I want to share some information with you about some new job responsibilities I have for you. I think you'll be happy about it."

"Yes, sir. Thank you, and I'll take care of it."

As his boss walked away, Juan felt more than a little bit giddy. Work was going well, and Darlene seemed like she wanted to stay around a while. All in all, he felt like things were looking up.

He got to his cubicle, and realized he couldn't sit still. He wanted to share his good news with someone, but not Dex this time. Juan wasn't in the mood for Dex's brand of sarcasm and attempted humor. He went to the break room. He found himself wanting to thank God for his opportunities. He had a somewhat more consistent prayer life throughout college, up to praying for this job. God answered the prayer abundantly and made Juan a good fit with the company. Pay raises and increased responsibility came in short order. With the success in the workplace, his prayer life stagnated. Early morning meetings and late night report writing sessions left him stressed and irritable. He started hitting the gym more consistently to fight off the physical effects of workplace stress, but didn't hit the prayer line.

He waited until a couple of ladies finished microwaving tea then after they left the breakroom, he closed his eyes. "Dear God, You've done it again. You keep blessing me. You know what I need long before I ask. I thank you for providing me this job and the opportunities that have come with it. Also, You allowed me to meet Darlene. Your grace and mercy are new every day. You are amazing. Thank You, Lord, for loving me so."

After he finished his prayer, Juan thought it would be a good time to call Darlene. He strolled back to his cubicle, grabbed his cell phone from the desk, and dialed her office number.

"This is Darlene Brown. I'm away from my desk. Please leave a short message with your number, and I will call you back. Goodbye and God bless you."

Juan left a message. "Darlene, this is Juan. You wanna hang out tonight? If so, game a call on my cell."

A few moments later, his cell phone buzzed. Darlene's cell number showed up on the screen. He cleared his throat, took a deep breath and answered. "Hey, you. Thanks for calling me back." Juan stammered a bit. He could feel himself starting to blush, and he was thankful that Darlene couldn't see him. Suddenly, in the midst of his awkwardness, he felt a flush of confidence. "I was thinking about you." He heard silence from the other end of the call. It only lasted a couple of beats, but to Juan it felt like this side of forever.

"Same here."

"Oh, yeah? Hey?"

"Yes, Juan?"

"There's a new museum not far from where you work. It has a small snack bar. How about meeting there for lunch?"

"That sounds good," she said.

'Cool," Juan blurted, which wasn't his usual style. He felt himself getting a little jazzy, a little full of himself. But, why not? Things were on the upswing. Why pretend to be a staid, low-key, closed-off guy when things were looking so bright? He told her where the museum was located and they agreed to meet at noon.

■

The clock over the door read 11:35. Juan felt relieved that he wasn't late. Being late, even the least bit, was a real pet peeve of his. He had a few moments to gather himself before Darlene arrived.

The Museum of Pop Culture and Sequential Art had only been open a few months. Juan tried it out during the opening week, and appreciated the convenience to the office. If nothing else, it would offer a change of pace from the usual catered grub that came into the office every day. The previous time he had come by, there was still some decorating tasks unfinished, so he didn't have a complete view of what the finished space would look like.

The museum ownership felt that this was a trendy opportunity, focusing on things readily familiar. Of course people would stop in to see displays of things they knew about, such as sitcoms and comic books. Some items were quite recent, but others dated back to the 1940s. To hedge their bets, the owners used some of the space for a Spartan-appointed snack bar. That way, even if a visitor happened not to like the choice of displays and artifacts, at least he or she could get a tasty snack.

Juan made his way to the snack bar just off to the side of the main entrance, taking a seat at a small oval table. A Spartan motif was evident along the walls, embossed on the menus, and even stenciled on the front doors. Unfortunately, the actual offerings didn't follow that theme. It might have been more interesting than what was actually offered.

The lunch menu included the usual deli sandwiches, small sides like potato salad and cole slaw, and a small selection of fruit and green salads. The food was good, and the selection of teas and other hot beverages was impressive. Teas from several countries abroad were available, all expertly served. Juan figured it was a matter of time before that info got out and this place would suddenly become crowded beyond belief. But, for now, it was an intimate setting. He hoped Darlene would be impressed.

Twelve o'clock came, and on cue Darlene walked in. He stood as she approached the small oval table where he sat. She had the most beautiful hazel eyes. He found himself staring a couple of beats longer than proper, but quickly caught himself. "It's good to see you. How has your day been so far?"

"Actually, pretty exciting. Local politics, crime and education are always issues that get people started up. I'll have several topics to consider later for my next column. What's up with you?"

It was an innocent question, but because of what was on his mind and heart, it struck him in a different place. He took a deep breath and started his confession. "Darlene, I enjoy your company. I'd like to enjoy it more on a regular basis. You, just you. You understand what I'm saying?"

Darlene let a small smile creep from her lips. She glanced outside, then back at Juan. She looked straight into his eyes. "Yeah, I understand. And maybe there can be something between us. I know we don't know everything about each other. You may get to know me and decide that you actually don't

121

want to know me any better. But in the meantime, let's see where this goes. I'm in. Now of course, if I find out you are some kinda drug kingpin or ax murderer, you can keep on moving and get away from me." She smirked, letting him know she was kidding.

Juan let out a large sigh of relief. He smiled his sweetest smile at Darlene. "I'm loyal," he said.

"Yeah, I can tell."

"I'm trustworthy," he added.

"I can see that too," she replied.

"I can be good for you and good to you."

"Juan, I get it. You don't have to try so hard. My answer is yes, I'll see you socially. You and you alone." Darlene absent-mindedly ran a finger along the edge of a menu set up on one side of the table. "Is this the reason you wanted to meet me mid-day?"

"What do you mean?" Juan asked.

"You know, just in case I said no, you would have an automatic reason to leave?" Darlene gave Juan the glance women give men when a man's plan is exposed.

"How did you guess?" Juan couldn't help but chuckle.

"I've paid attention to people over the years. And, if things didn't go well, you had a built-in escape plan. Makes sense to me. But, since we have agreed to date, you have no reason to escape now, do you?" Darlene took Juan's hand in hers. He couldn't help but notice just how soft her skin was, but also how firm her grip was. "I'm looking forward to seeing where this goes."

Juan gave her hands a squeeze in return. "So am I." He looked at the clock on the wall. Fifteen minutes had gone by, and his life had just changed in a profound manner. He was now paired up with somebody. Somebody intelligent, beautiful, and desirable in every way. "Hey, I have an idea. Tell me what you think about this. Let's take a night, tonight in fact."

"Go ahead, I'm listening."

"Let's take the time to pray about this. See how God wants us to run this situation."

"Oh, we're now some kind of situation? I thought we were dating now."

Juan rolled his eyes. "You know what I mean. Of course we're dating. But anyway, I think we should sit down and consider what we need out of a relationship. Don't write a book, but jot down a few things that are concerns to each of us. Things that could be deal breakers. Things that we want to make sure get said before we get too far down the road."

"Juan, I hear you. Don't know about you, but I have been in a couple of near-almost-relationships over the years and as things ended, there were all sorts of things I wish I'd said but didn't get the chance to say. Now, maybe some of those topics will get covered the right way."

"I agree big-time, and I'm not going to hit you up with things I'm angry about concerning previous women. What they did or didn't do wasn't your fault, and I won't blame you for their mess, alright?"

"Sure. I'll do the same for you, alright?"

"Alright." Juan smiled at his new special lady and glanced again at the clock. It would soon be time for him to get back to work.

"I'm sooooo glad we got to talk for a bit. In the meantime, are you hungry or thirsty? You want to get something quick? I've only been here once, but the egg salad sandwich is pretty good."

"Hungry, no. Thirsty, yeah. I could go for something. Hot tea would hit the spot."

"I'll go place the order." Juan rose from the table and headed up front. Darlene watched him walk away and thought to herself that her new boyfriend was decent to look at, a decent-enough dresser and didn't appear to have any weird mannerisms. He could be someone she could take places. *Yeah,* Darlene thought, *this just might work.*

The remainder of their lunch rendezvous was pleasant. Darlene and Juan shared a few laughs, worked their respective beverages, and had a nice time. Some of the initial, *I've gotta impress you at all costs* tension was gone, and replaced by a growing ease between the two of them.

Juan couldn't help but notice that the mood changed faster than he expected, and much smoother as well. He hated to leave Darlene, but work beckoned. "I'd better head back to the shop. Can I walk you to your car?"

"Why, yes, you can. I'd like it. It's one of those special moments, after all."

The newly-minted couple headed out the door, with Juan opening it for Darlene. They went out into the brilliant sunshine. Darlene reached into her purse for a pair of sunglasses.

Juan noticed that Darlene carried herself with a real sense of poise and class in everything she did. As they walked down the street to where Darlene was parked, Juan felt a sense of pride and wariness. Pride regarding the fact that he was now dating a lady that other men found attractive. Wariness in the fact that perhaps she was the type of girl who maybe enjoyed the attention too much. Juan made a mental note to bring that up at their next meeting, the one when they would go over their respective relationship concerns.

"Something on your mind, Juan? You seem quiet all of a sudden."

"Nah, I'm good. I'll call you tonight."

"You know, I'm looking forward to getting to know you better. You got a bunch of potential. Maybe I'm the one to help you reach more of it."

"You helping me sounds like fun," Juan agreed.

"I like the way you think."

CHAPTER 23

Juan arrived to the gym in time for a spin class. He rode like a madman for fifty minutes. One thing crossed his mind, which was he was going to refrain from pursuing Darlene sexually. He had gone down that road numerous times before, and in the end none of the liaisons evolved into anything lasting and mutually satisfying. It seemed like once sex happened, the preconceived notions kicked in. In the past, he or the lady automatically inserted expectations into the relationship. Those expectations fueled disagreements of opinion, which in turn led to heavy arguments, and finally the realization that the relationship was doomed. This time, he was determined to deal with Darlene in a purposeful sense. No guesswork, no fumbling around. He didn't want regrets nor confusion. Things may or may not work out – only God knew for sure. But, at least this time the lady was gonna get the best he had to offer.

The more he thought about what could take place between him and Darlene, the more he looked forward to getting to know more about her. With Darlene, he didn't feel like he had to put on a façade to impress her. He felt that he could be himself. He wasn't going to bet his self-worth on whether or not she found him sexually appealing. She would have to learn about him in a different way, and they both would figure out if things were going to work out. Before he realized it, class was over. He had spent nearly the whole fifty-minutes thinking about Darlene. He had to chuckle to himself, since he hadn't thought this hard about a female in a while.

He dismounted the bike and commenced with his post-ride stretching. He wasn't completely ripped, but he was fit enough to be presentable. He allowed himself a small amount of ego, thinking at least she wouldn't be embarrassed to be seen with him out in public.

He gathered his gym bag and headed out of the room. At other times, he might have taken a moment to catch the eye of some female who'd also been in the class, but this time, he didn't feel obligated to check for prospects. That, to him, was a good feeling.

Meanwhile in another part of town, Darlene worked on her next column. She loved her work, and enjoyed the feeling of using her gifts to draw attention to the ills of local society. As she was in the flow of thought, her mind ever so often drifted to Juan. He really did seem like a man with a lot on the ball, and she looked forward to talking to him later that night.

When she got off work that evening, she was a bit hungry. Once she arrived home, she gathered the necessary items to prepare breakfast-for-dinner. She looked in the fridge. There were a few eggs, some smoked sausage and some strawberry jam.

The food she prepared was tasty and satisfying. With her laptop fired up, she started working on the list she was going to share with Juan. This was a unique opportunity. Instead of reacting to a man she barely knew or finding surprises that may or may not be worthwhile, she could take a smarter approach in dealing with a man romantically. She wouldn't repeat the same mistakes she had made with Grant.

Now that Darlene found herself in Juan's life, she wondered if he would be as needy as Grant was.

CHAPTER 24

Juan gathered his wits. He hadn't felt this nervous in a long time, but it wasn't dread as much as anticipation. This was a chance to have a real relationship, and he wanted to get it off to the right start. He reached for his phone, took a deep breath, and dialed Darlene's number.

"Hey, there."

"Hey, there," Darlene said. "It's nice to hear your voice."

"How is your day so far?"

"Good. What about yours?"

"It's been cool but uneventful."

"Have you been working on your list?"

"Yeah, I have. Wassup?" Juan asked.

"I was thinking, it wouldn't hurt to have a backup. Since we both have work Monday, I figure we can start on this list thing now and follow up in the days and nights to come."

"Ummm. Days and nights to come? That sounds good. So, let's crank up this list thing. You ready?"

"Yeah. I'm ready. Do you mind if I put out a couple of ideas before we start?" Darlene added.

"Don't mind at all. Bring it on."

"First off, I want to state that I understand that people change and evolve as stuff like work, health, family, etc., impact their lives. So, some of the stuff on the list may evolve with the changes in our lives. Make sense?"

"Yeah, I get it."

"Also, my pledge to you is that whatever I ask you to do I need to do the same, or at least have the same intent. That goes for the stuff we're about to cover tonight, too. That makes sense also?"

"Sure, and that sounds good. Hey, do you have any plans for dinner?" Juan asked.

"Not really.

"Would you like to meet up somewhere, or better yet, I could bring some take out by your place and we can work on our list."

"You know, takeout sounds good. You need my address though. Let me know when you're ready."

"Always ready. Go for it."

"I'm at 7577 Rivera Lane, near the intersection of Baldwin Boulevard and Scott Street."

"I know that area. I can be there by six-thirty. What do you have a taste for?"

"I'm pretty flexible. Just so you know, I'm not a big fan of red meat. I'm more of a chicken and seafood kind of guy. I like Chinese, too."

"Okay, then I know the perfect place. I'll pick up dinner for two and see ya at six-thirty."

Darlene chuckled and so did Juan. "See ya shortly."

"Later." Juan felt a smile creep across his face. It felt good to have a lady who wanted to spend time with him and him alone. *Wow,* he thought. *Not a bad deal at all.*

■

"Welcome to my home. Thanks for bringing dinner." Juan took Darlene in his arms and found she fit nicely. With each heartbeat, it became increasingly difficult to let her go. He felt a bit light-headed.

Darlene was in no hurry to escape his embrace. Even with the bags of takeout, she was content in his arms. Finally, he let her go, helped her with the bags, and the couple worked their way towards the kitchen.

They sat at the kitchen table. Juan took Darlene's hands into his own; they both bowed their heads, closed their eyes, and thanked God for the food and the fellowship.

The new couple munched on appetizers while getting comfortable with one another.

"Good chow, baby. I love it. Where is this place located?"

"Actually, a few blocks west of here. Small, out-of-the-way place. Good grub, reasonable prices."

"I hear ya." Juan finished off an egg roll and reached in one of the bags for the main course. Shrimp lo mien and combination fried rice were the night's choices, accompanied by steamed vegetables. He grabbed the container of fried rice and offered first dibs to Darlene. She nodded, and he served her a small portion. She nodded at him to ask for more. He obliged.

"So, are you putting on a show for my benefit, to impress me and get me to like you more?"

"Aw, baby. You know that ain't it. I want to impress you, sure. But not to hustle you for this or that."

"Awww, it makes me feel good that you want to impress little ol' me. But if you really want to impress me, then do right by God first, foremost and always. A Godly man is impressive in all he does."

Juan mulled over Darlene's statement. He'd never thought about the extent of commitment necessary to truly walk in God's will. And, based on Darlene's view, if he did ramp up his commitment, would he only be doing it to impress her? *That can't be the main reason to serve the Lord,* he thought. He muttered a half-hearted, "I got ya." That exchange gave him more to think about.

The rest of the meal was pleasant. Juan noticed as Darlene opened up to him, she shared a depth of character that only a few people saw. There were plenty of laughs, some sharing of some fears and frustrations, and an overall sense of two spirits and hearts meshing. The initial nervousness he felt in hosting her dissolved, in large part due to her warmth. Juan was reluctant to call it love at that moment, but the attraction was strong and growing.

The night went by quickly. Soon, it was ten o'clock. "Hey, I'm really enjoying this, but it's getting late. I better leave before I get too attached." Darlene stood up from her seat, yawned and stretched.

As she stood there, Juan got a chance to see her in full bloom. To him, she was an exceptionally beautiful woman. She had an accompanying grace that hit him deep in his heart. When he took in her beauty, he was pretty much speechless.

Darlene noticed him staring. "You ok? You seem like the cat got your tongue." Darlene smiled sweetly at Juan, and his heart melted a little more.

"Oh, I'm fine. Just digging you. In our haste to get to know one another, I'm just now taking the time to see just how beautiful you are. I gotta admit, I don't think I've ever seen a woman as dazzling as you. Ever."

"Well, your flattery is appreciated. You're not so bad yourself. You're a good-looking man, well-groomed and fit. You'll do, you'll do quite nicely." She smiled.

"But, I want to be sure that we know each other well enough before we go further."

"Juan, I'm not pressuring you for a long-term commitment, so you have nothing to worry about. I'm with you; let's take the time to learn about what we're getting into. If down the road we feel that God is supporting us into something deeper, then we'll deal with that when it happens. In the meantime, I look forward to this journey."

Juan was at once encouraged and a bit stunned. Encouraged by her confidence in the possibility of them growing closer, stunned at the view that she saw places where he could grow. However, he didn't speak up on his concern.

Darlene noticed a subtle shift in his body language. "Did that throw you off? I didn't mean to offend you, but I really believe we all have places to grow. I don't know the places where you feel you need growth. That's between you and God. However, I think you and I would agree that as every day goes by, if we're paying attention, there are things we can learn. Things we can adapt for our own lives. I certainly believe that and live by it. God shows me something every day. Sometimes those things are big deal things. Sometimes, they're subtle things that I miss if I don't shut up. If I take time to listen, God wants to reveal good, useful stuff to me. What do you think?"

"Yeah, I agree. Guess I run around too much and don't pay enough attention. I probably have missed some good stuff God wanted to show me."

"Yeah, I hear ya. Well, that's my view at least." Darlene looked at her watch, and started working her way towards the door. "Keep the leftovers. And, since you'll be taking me out next time, we'll be even on the whole who treats who stuff. Gunfight, good man. I'll talk to you tomorrow." Darlene rose up on her tippy-toes, wrapped her arms around Juan's neck, and gave him a short and sweet kiss on the lips.

Her lips were soft and tasty. He kissed her again.

"I'll walk you to your car." As Juan opened the door for Darlene, he looked at the nighttime sky. A crescent of a waning moon shone overhead. Stars twinkled and planets offered reflected glow. It was a beautiful night, and he had his arm around the shoulder of a beautiful lady. She seemed relaxed at his side.

"Nice night, eh?"

"Yeah. You know if we were kids, this would be a great night to stay out past bedtime. Don't know about your past, but I grew up in neighborhoods that were fairly quiet. Once in a while, during the summer months, my parents would let us stay out well after dark. We carried on like lunatics, running around in circles, playing hide and seek, and other stuff. And, the times we went to my grandparents' farm, we could count the stars and planets, while slapping at mosquitoes and gnats."

"That sounds like fun," Darlene said. "We couldn't do that in my neighborhood. We lived in a pretty rough area. Every once in a while, if my parents were around and wanted to, they would sit on the porch and make small talk. They would let me go out in our yard but no further. When we were little, a couple of cartwheels would be enough. Maybe some hopscotch. When I got too cool for cartwheels, I would sit on the porch and listen to them talk about the events of the day."

"Is that where you got your desire to become a reporter? To deal with the issues of the day?"

"Yeah, in part. You know how it goes though. As I became a teenager, every once in a while I would get bold and express myself. The conversations were pretty intriguing, so they made time to do it more often as time went on."

"Dang, that's kinda bold, Darlene. My folks would've shut me down immediately if I had tried that."

"I hear ya. I didn't realize this until I got older, but adults don't have to indulge young people in grown-up conversation. To their credit, my parents didn't shut me down. They took those times to pass on small bites of insight. They would engage me as an equal, sometimes of course, to ensure I had not only a greater understanding on an issue but to also ensure I did my homework before I could participate in their conversations."

"Wow, that sounds pretty cool."

"Yeah. Looking back, that was pretty generous of them. Given that, I got used to reading the paper from front page to back page. Major stories, want ads, comics, personals. I devoured it all."

They got to Darlene's car and Juan opened the door, watched her take the driver's seat, and closed the door behind her. He couldn't help but smile. He took a couple of steps back from the driveway and watched her back her car out into the street. He lingered next to his driveway until her car's tail lights disappeared around a corner.

Juan recognized that recurring lightness in his spirit. Darlene was quite different from previous girls he'd dated. For the previous few years, he had learned to be gracious on dates, but not get his hopes up too high. The girls he was attracted to didn't seem to want to make the same effort in getting to know him as he was expected to make in pursuing them.

Darlene seemed to actively want to know him better and hear what he thought. Maybe the timing was right, where he was attracted to the lady the same time the lady was attracted to him. It was a nice place to be.

Juan went inside, locked his front door, and then heard his phone buzz. He picked it up and looked at the screen. It was Dex.

"Juan, yo, bro. How does it go?"

"Dex, wassup man? Lemme guess. You want a download on me and Darlene. Hey, wait a minute," Juan stammered.

"C'mon, brother. It's me, Dex. I was here at the house watching a game, thought you had seen some of the same highlights, called you to give you some grief about it, noticed you didn't pick up when I called, and just guessed you were with your girl. Now, given the local time and the fact that you picked up the phone this time, I would guess she isn't there now."

"Yeah. It is a work night, after all."

"Wow, you let her go this early? You didn't take her hostage or anything? You know, I wouldn't have let a lady leave that early without spending some uh, private time with ol' Dex."

"Yeah, I hear ya. But, like I touched on before, I want to do things differently this time. In my spirit, deep down, I know it's right."

"Oh, yeah? How do you know that exactly?"

"Dex, think about it. All these times, all these years. You've done it, I've tried to do it. Meet a girl. Hit and run. Not looking back. Not being concerned about what or who we leave behind. We're not even talking about the times when we got shot down in the clubs."

"Juan, that's just life man. No sense in over-thinking this thing. That's just the way things are."

"Nah, I can't settle for that. Dude, we're not teenagers anymore. This isn't some sort of playground where we play with peoples' hearts and lives."

"You need to lighten up, man. Life is too short."

"Don't miss my point. It seemed clearer just now. God made men and women different on purpose, to complement one another. Like two pieces of a puzzle, they're different shapes, literally and figuratively, but they fit together because they're supposed to."

Dex stammered for a response, but couldn't think of anything coherent.

"Look, Dex. I'm not your dad. In no way am I trying to tell you how to live your life. But for me, there's got to be a better way than the back and forth we go through these days. I'm tired of dealing with women where it seems that no sooner than you meet the clock is already running. It's just a matter of time before things end. There has to be a better way, a more rewarding way, to deal with women."

"I understand that you want Darlene to see the best of you. I get it, I really do. It's a natural thing to want to impress your lady, but I think it's a move that's destined to fail."

"What do you mean?"

"Dude, if you give her the impression that you'll jump through a hoop now, there will always be another hoop. Once you start down that road, it never ends," Dex warned. "You won't have enough time in your day to jump through every hoop that she puts in your path."

"Darlene isn't that way. In the little bit of time she and I have hung out, she shows something unique from the girls we met before. That's one of the things that I really like about her. I don't think she'll react like girls we already know. Actually, I'm looking forward to finding out more about her, especially without the after-sex expectations. You, of all people, ought to know about those expectations."

"Oh, yeah. I know about them. I just don't pay them any mind, that's all."

"But don't you think there's a reason for the expectations? Don't you think that when we take that step of intimacy, that it's only natural for the man or the woman, or both, to expect

139

something deeper? Something more than just being dropped off at the end of the night?"

"I hear what you're saying. It makes sense, it really does. But, you can't expect the world around us to change just because you have gained new insight," Dex said.

"I don't expect the world to change. But I have to."

"Let me finish, bro. Not only can you not expect the world to change, perhaps you can't even expect one person to change. Maybe you can't expect Darlene to change. After all, you don't know her all that well. She may be going along with you for now, to show you her best side. But, let something hit her in a sensitive place. Maybe something about her looks. Maybe some other woman makes eye contact with you and her insecurities surface. Then, the lady may think that you haven't made a move because you just aren't attracted to her. Then the argument starts. 'Do you not find me attractive?' she asks. 'Of course I find you attractive,' you respond. 'Well, why don't you, you know, come on to me. Other guys act like they wanna get with their girls. What's wrong with me that you don't act that way?' Then you respond, 'I'm not other guys. I'm trying to treat you better than that'. You think that approach is gonna work, and it very well might. But you getting creative in a relationship, to me, opens you up to the thing not working. And you know me. I've attempted to play a role. Some of the women were actually pretty impressive.

Beauty, smarts, home training. At the time, I was moving way too fast to notice what they were going through. You may have noticed that many of the women I met at Frisky's didn't come back to hang out after I let 'em go."

"Now that you mention it, you didn't seem to have a lot of repeat business."

"Interesting way to put it, Juan. Maybe I was wrong. Maybe I actually hurt women who didn't deserve to be hurt. But, I can't go back to make it right, make amends. Those women were grown; they made grown-up choices, and they had good times as well."

"Can you be sure of that, Dex? Do you really know, or do you think that they were playing a role? Do you think that maybe they didn't want much out of you but a good time for a short period? If that's the case, where you both were playing roles at the same time, manoman, that sounds like an empty way to live. I don't think I could hang in a situation like that, wondering if she really wanted to be with me, or if she was just passing time until a better situation came up."

"So, Juan. What's a reasonable alternative? I hear what you're saying and what you're trying to accomplish. But, given the world in which we live, where the majority of people don't think like you, how do you expect things to work out? You know me, you can do whatever you want and I'll try to find a way to make a joke out of it. That's just what I do. But, from one friend to another, I wouldn't be a friend if I didn't at least attempt to warn you not to get your hopes up too much. You have this big hope about things with you and Darlene going rational and reasonable. But you and I both know the streets. She can be a church girl and still end up pulling something that'll make you wonder."

"Dex, I hear ya. I realize that this world gets crazier with every passing day. Things seem cool now, but I wouldn't be me if I didn't at least try to plant the seed early on. Set the stage where she and I can head off a lot of the arguments, disagreements, and differences of opinion. Right now, at least, it seems like Darlene wants to work with me, meet me halfway on stuff. If that continues to be the case, we can have some great times. I think I want that with her."

"So, with that, do you think that she is long-term potential? Do you think you want to keep her around in your life for a while? 'cause you know if that's the case, there's a big word that has to come up."

"What word is that?"

"Matrimony. Sooner or later, you and I both know she'll be compelled to ask you what you see for the two of you down the road. You in for the duration, or what?' I know it probably won't come up tomorrow, or next week, but it will come up, and you need to be ready to give an answer."

"Dex, you're getting way too ahead of yourself. Darlene and I don't know enough about each other, about our backgrounds, to where we can even start to talk about that. Right now, I want to find out more about her. She's cool to hang out with, cool to talk with, and you know she's cool to look at. She has a lot of great qualities and she seems to feel similar towards me. Soooo, I wanna go down this road a bit, see what it looks like. After all, I'm not getting younger. I'm kind of getting to the point where settling down sounds enjoyable. Next step is finding the right lady. If Darlene isn't the one, cool."

"I hear ya, and I hope it works out. All I'm saying is don't fool yourself. Keep your eyes open."

"I hear what you're saying. But I got this."

Dex yawned a yawn that evoked either a jungle animal or a guy who didn't care what other people thought about his lack of social graces. He figured this was a great point to end the conversation. "Alright, man. Time to call it. I'll talk to you down the road, bro."

"You right. Look, man. I'm fading. I'll catch ya later, bro."

■

Darlene drove home feeling light-hearted. She didn't want to get ahead of herself, but she felt more and more that Juan was a man with considerable potential.

As she pulled up at her home, she realized she wasn't sleepy. She parked, checked her surroundings, asked God for safety leaving her car and entering her house, got out of the car and went inside.

Since she was going to be up for a bit, Darlene microwaved a mug of water for tea. After hearing the familiar ding, she removed the mug from the microwave and dipped in a bag of green tea for steeping.

She went into the bedroom and changed into her favorite fuzzy pajamas.

Darlene hadn't felt this giddy about a guy ever in her life, and it actually scared her a bit. It was a similar feeling to standing at the top of a tall building—the view was striking, but the risk was real. She didn't relish the potential for a long fall ending in a crushing landing. The chance to enjoy a perch high above the troubles and nonsense on the street was bracing. She didn't want to admit this to anyone, but the girlish heart in her wanted this relationship with Juan to work. She wanted to keep things grounded, and not lose herself in the heady rush of new attraction.

After she finished her tea, she went to her bedroom. and dropped to her knees to pray.

After praying, she slipped under her covers and turned off her lamp. Dozing off quickly, Darlene found herself at peace, dreaming about Juan. Nothing big or life-changing, but being at peace with him. The two of them were out and about spending time together. She didn't remember a lot of details, but she did remember in the dream seeing her left hand without a ring. She rarely wore jewelry anyway,

but this time seeing her hand ringless stood
out as noticeable.

CHAPTER 25

Wednesday, "Hump Day" as some people called it. Juan got to work in one piece and dove into the tasks of the day. Although many in his office seemed to drag mid-week, he looked forward to Wednesdays. He saw it as a chance to set himself apart from his peers, taking on challenges others tried to avoid. Whether it was a meeting, a position package recommending action, or a summary of recently completed tasks with possible outcomes, any task could be that item that set him apart in the eyes of his bosses. Although he didn't broadcast it, he was quite ambitious. He felt destined to move up the corporate ladder as swiftly as possible. He didn't want to step on anyone on the way up, since he really believed what his parents taught him about meeting the same people on the way up as he would on the way down. He suspected that he wouldn't get many chances to achieve success and there would also be a time when the company would let him know in a not-very-compassionate way that his services were no longer needed. With all that, Juan was convinced he had to be impressive in the workplace every single day. After all, this was one way he graded himself as a man – his competence at his profession.

By ten o'clock, Juan was in a real groove. His observational skills and coordination with other offices and functions were clicking. People he called responded promptly to his requests for information. His immediate superiors got info they needed from him in a timely fashion. Even secretaries and admin assistants greeted him warmly when he approached them. It was a great day in the workplace.

As he took a quick coffee break, Juan got a call from Darlene.

"Mister White Collar Professional, how are you this morning?"

"Queen of Intrepid Journalism, I'm well. It's good to hear your voice. Did you get enough sleep last night?"

"Why, yes I did. It wasn't a lot of hours, but it was very restorative. And, guess what I dreamed about, or should I say who?"

"I have no idea," Juan said lightly.

"It was you, you and me."

"Ahhh, and what exactly were we doing?" Juan asked.

"We were walking along Peterson Park, having a good time in each other's company."

"Mmmm, sounds good. I look forward to the real thing."

"Yeah, me too. Do you ever remember your dreams?"

"I do but I rarely remember all of the details. Usually, when the alarm goes off, whatever I was dreaming about fades away."

"You know what? You ought to keep a journal next to your bed, so when you do dream, if you remember anything at all, you can write it down. You may find some insight about yourself. Maybe, just maybe, I could be coerced to pick up a journal for you."

"Sounds interesting. I won't stop you if you were to do something like that."

"Sure thing. For you, I would be happy to do it. Hey, there's something I want to bounce off you before you go back to work."

"Go for it."

"Earlier today, some of the staff writers got into a long, drawn-out discussion about how stereotypes and misunderstandings get in the way of folk understanding each other. What I was thinking was this. I could make dinner for us one night, you come over, and we sit down and take turns sharing our views on the different stereotypes. Maybe we can understand each other better and break down stuff that might get in our way. What do you think?"

"Sounds like a good idea. There are some questions about your gender that I want to understand. In turn, I could tell you secrets of manhood that you ladies may want to know. All I ask is that when you tell your women friends and acquaintances manly secrets, you don't attribute me as your source."

"Manly secrets. Oooh. Sounds juicy. I really look forward to it."

"I do too. I look forward to you. What do you plan on cooking?"

"I don't know, but it'll be light. Any special requests?"

"Well, you've seen what I like. Now that I think about it, I don't like stuffed peppers and cauliflower."

"Well, my specialty twice-baked cauliflower stuffed peppers is out."

"There is such a thing? You can't be serious."

"C'mon now, you know me. I'm a kidder from time to time. Nah, there isn't such a thing. At least not that I know of, but, now that you mention it."

"Hey now. I don't want any credit or association with that. Sounds kinda nasty, and I don't want my name next to it at all."

"I hear ya. No cauliflower or stuffed peppers a la Juan. Copy all." They both giggled.

"I'm gonna get back at it, but I appreciate you calling. Your voice is soothing, and a real lift on an already rockin' day."

"That's nice of you to say, sweetie. Hey, are you going to Bible Study tonight? If so, can I ride with you?"

"I'm not sure just yet. I have a late afternoon meeting, so it might be close, time-wise."

"I understand. Gimme a call when you know for sure. See ya later, sweetie."

"Okay, later." As Juan hung up, the word sweetie echoed in his ears. He didn't anticipate things going this far this fast. He enjoyed the fact that Darlene seemed to like him a little more with each passing day. Even as he hung up the phone, he had to fight back the urge to either call her back up right away or run to be by her side.

CHAPTER 26

Peterson Park was in the center of the city. Named after a resident who was a bomber commander in World War II, it was a pastoral setting in the midst of an otherwise hectic, grungy downtown. The city fathers were determined to keep this patch of green untouched. At the risk of the park seemingly under siege, there always seemed to be a marked police patrol car cruising the grounds. Many residents suspected the police department detached a few plainclothes officers to that location as well. The mere rumor of such kept a lot of the hooliganism to a minimum. So, there was a preternatural calm to the park, which made it a nice meeting place for Darlene and Candi Stephenson. The time was three minutes after noon. Darlene and Candi met one another at the entrance to the park.

"Sorry for being late, Candi. The line at the store was longer than usual, even for lunch customers."

"Don't sweat it. I bought apple cake. Hope that isn't too heavy for a mid-day snack."

"Nah, no problem. I'll just walk it off, stretch it off, whatever."

"So you're saying that you lose weight by stretching, Darlene? Go on, get oughtta here. I can't believe that."

"Not by itself, but in combination with other things. Anyway, thanks for bringing this. Here's a bottle of *agua* to wash it down." Darlene offered Candi a chilled bottle of water before taking one for herself.

Candi took the bottle, nodded thanks and twisted the cap off. "Ok, girlie. Tell me more about this Juan guy."

"Well, Lemme see. He has a sense of poise. Seems to be a real classy guy, patient too, and he has a great sense of humor. Seems to have been taught how to treat a lady. Maybe he got that from his family. I haven't met them yet. Reinforcing the abstinence piece was a pleasant surprise. Maybe he really wants to get to know me for who I am."

"All that sounds good, at least at first glance."

"Yeah. I gotta say, Candi, I've never met a guy like him. He's almost naïve in not realizing just how much Godly potential is in him."

"Unique is good, for what it's worth. How much do you know about what goes on in his head?"

"Well, I don't know anything about his family. That troubles me a little. He never talks about them. At least not to this point."

"Well, it hasn't been that long since the two of you met. What have you told him about yours?"

"Bits and pieces. We've been spending lots of time with each other, but I guess we really haven't made the effort to dig into our pasts."

"Hope you don't get any crazy surprises."

"You mean like he was a former lottery winner or a gunrunner?"

Candi snorted out a chuckle. "Or maybe he was a child actor in the old days."

"Yeah, and that was him I saw in that one sci-fi movie when I was in college! He was the kid who saved the world from the bug-eyed monsters." Darlene cracked herself up at the absurdity.

Candi had to restrain herself the midst of her convulsive laughter. "I hear ya. But now that we have figured out a part of his past, we ought to consider the near future. The real near future."

"Yeah, you got that right," Darlene readily agreed.

"What about his walk with Christ? How is his faith? How much more has he shared?"

"He seems like he believes. We haven't talked about our respective salvation experiences yet. He also seems to be more active seeking out Bible Study opportunities and other fellowships. In my spirit, I get the impression he is more a seeker than one who has plateaued."

"Well, you definitely want to take some time with him, sooner rather than later, and talk that part out. You don't want to get down the road with this guy, thinking he is saved and a strong believer, then discover some issue or incident that makes him show his lack of faith."

"Yeah, you got that right as well."

"There is something else I want to bring up, before I forget."

"Oh, yeah? What's that?"

"Over the years, I've heard so many women saying 'the man has to do this for me' or 'the man has to do that for me or I won't waste time on him'. In the meantime, the women aren't saying what they are willing to give to the man. And, no, I'm not talking about sex. My advice is, be real careful about what you demand from Juan. You may find yourself compelled to answer the same question when it's directed to you," Candi advised.

"Yeah, I know. What's good for the goose is truly good for the gander. But, what about when the man jumps up and says the woman has to look like this, or has to be a size two when he has hoagies and beer with his boys every weekend after work?"

"Darlene, that part sometimes happens as well. Lord knows, none of our hands are clean when it comes to failing relationships. Men and women are guilty, many times, at the same time. Maybe one person or the other ends up with more blame, depending on who writes the post-mortem. But both are responsible, both had a role in planting the early seeds for success or failure. The general question for you two is what seeds will you plant now?"

Darlene mulled over the advice. She had long trusted Candi on a lot of life issues. "So, you're saying whatever I demand of Juan, I better be ready to do the same, or nearly the same."

"Bingo. You get it. You win another piece of apple cake."

"I feel like a winner right about now. I may have to take that slice with me and have it later."

"How long have we known one another?"

"A little over two years, if I recollect correctly."

"I don't want to overload you with a lot of words. A lot of this, whether it's Juan or whomever, you'll have to see for yourself. And also, it's not like I'm in a successful relationship that can be a model for you."

"Candi, you and I both know that you've helped keep me on track since we met. I've seen the fruit of your walk with the Lord, and I have been blessed by it also. I hear you completely, and I'm taking this in."

"You're sweet and kind, young lady. I just want to see you content in God's will for your life. Maybe this is the time for you to have a relationship. I, in no way, want to tell you how to go day by day with Juan, but I wouldn't be your friend if I didn't at least offer a chance to be a sounding board.

Candi took a long draw of water followed by a bite of apple cake, then furrowed her brow. "I don't want to overload you now, and I know you have to get back to your office. But, I wanna share a few more things before we part. How do you argue?"

"I usually see both sides on an issue. Don't normally raise my voice. I get it when others have different views. I can disagree without hating the person with a different view."

"All righty. Sounds like you get it to me. My suggestion was gonna be, make sure you learn how to separate the person from the position. So often I run across people who feel they have to win every argument. They could be as wrong as two left shoes, but don't want to relinquish their ego-driven position. To me, the ability to argue a point is a lost art among most people. I'm not saying roll over on an issue just to keep things peaceful, or being any person's doormat. You can stand strong and be fair without resorting to irrational anger."

"You got that right. I'm glad you said it out loud. Others could stand to hear it."

"Good thing for you, Darlene, is you get a chance to apply what you know. Also, maybe just maybe, you get to be a Godly example for others following in your footsteps. Maybe you and Juan will become leaders for a new movement. Keep it clean, keep it respectful and affectionate, let God be the one running your relationship. Given that, it doesn't necessarily matter what the short-term destination becomes for you two, as long as the both of you are obedient to the Lord's way."

"Candi, that is a great point. In no way do I expect or demand Juan to start talking about marriage or anything like that. I don't want to drive him away, but I don't want to mislead him either."

"Funny you should mention that. What do you expect from him?"

"What do you mean?"

"Either you're getting to know one another to see if a romantic relationship is in the offing, or the actual wooing towards a long-term relationship or marriage, preferably the latter. In no way do I mean that you are to box him in a corner. Don't force the issue. The time will be right when it comes up, and you will know it. It's perfectly okay to find out what he intends for you two. He ought to be man enough to have an idea about it. He may even be thinking about the same right now."

"He seems focused on his career. I haven't quizzed him about it, but I wonder about his list of priorities. How God, his work, me and whatever else he has going gets racked and stacked. I can take it if he puts God first. That's how it oughtta be. I don't need to be first priority to him, but I don't want to be fourth or fifth. I gotta know I mean something to him. Know what I mean?"

"All you gotta do is pay attention. He'll show you. Warning though, the same goes for you. Where you put him on your list of priorities will directly determine just how interested he stays in chasing you."

"He isn't chasing me. That's my fault. I should have made him wait some before I started claiming him."

"Yeah, maybe that's true. However, his willingness to get to know you without pressuring you for sex is a big risk for him. Some women would get all insecure if the guy didn't press the issue."

157

"What do you mean? Are you saying most women are really that shallow?"

"That's exactly what I'm saying. Then, the two find out that they can't get along, but the physical intimacy line has already been crossed. It's tough for either party to let go, is all I'm saying. Good thing you don't have to deal with that."

"Yeah, you got that right. But, Candi, I still want to be pursued. I still want to see that he's willing to go to some length, some effort of finding out about me."

Candi nodded her understanding and glanced at her watch. Lunch hour was almost over. "Well, missy, looks like lunch time is over. I'd better wrap things up and let you go. If you wanna talk or bounce an idea off me, feel free to call anytime."

"You know I will. I really appreciate you sharing some insight. There is so much about Juan that I don't know."

"He's worrying about the same regarding you, kiddo. Now, help me gather this stuff so we can get out of here."

CHAPTER 27

Juan found himself stuck in the middle of a disorganized, bureaucratically frustrating workday afternoon. Meetings ran long with minimal productivity. He looked at the clock on the wall – a quarter after four. With at least three hours of report drafting ahead of him, he decided to work as much as he could, but still try to break away in time to go pick up his girlfriend for Bible Study. Now that they were a couple, time together in Bible Study would be a great way to strengthen their bond. Splitting the difference between working the relationship and staying on the fast track at work was a new issue for him to juggle.

"Juan, the boss needs to see you." Normally, when the secretary used those words, Juan felt a rush, a chance to show his competence and creativity. Now, there was a twinge of , "I hope he doesn't add more work. I gotta get out of here in a bit."

Of course, the boss added more work. Bosses did that sometimes. The level of detail required on the earlier assignment was to be ratcheted up a notch. Also, the updated package of info was to be sent up-channel to higher echelons of company leadership. This would be a big deal, due first thing the next morning. That direction meant more research and more tweaking of the presentation to reflect the greater level of detail. Now, it was pretty much a foregone conclusion that there was no way he would be able to get out of the office early enough to pick up Darlene and get to church, even if he left some work undone until morning. Juan attentively copied his boss's insight, nodded affirmation, and hustled off to his workspace. He needed to alert his co-workers before they departed for the evening. Some of them had experience and insight that would prove crucial in getting this task done on time.

Naturally, as Juan divided the piece-part tasks and sat at his desk to work his portion, the phone rang. Darlene was on the line.

"Hi, baby. It's me. How goes it?"

"It goes, but it goes slowly. How are you?"

"I'm good. Had lunch with Candi, one of the triplets, remember?"

"Yeah, I remember. She's the leader, right?"

"Yeah, I guess you could say that. Maybe there's something to that birth order thing after all, you think?"

Juan chuckled a bit. "Yeah, maybe. Hey, I got bad news. Work is piling up. Big presentation my boss is making tomorrow morning, so I gotta finish a draft report tonight. I won't be able to make Bible Study."

"Wow, it is a small world, Juan. I have a short-notice job-related event too. Some local journalists' coalition meeting. We have to meet after work. I will be done before Bible study ends, but I won't be able to get there for the start. That's why I called, so you wouldn't rush to pick me up and find I wasn't at home."

"You're so sweet and considerate. Much thanks to you."

"Yeah, I am at that. God's grace and mercy, don'tcha know. Tell you what, though. I can get the notes from Candi or one of her sisters and we can go over them tomorrow night. What do you think? You available tomorrow night?"

"Sure. I look forward to hanging with you. Hey, can I tell you something?"

"Tell away."

"I was a bit nervous before you called. Didn't think you would be this understanding. I appreciate your cutting me some slack."

"Juan, I understand. I really do. But, literally you are putting this before God. Just like I am with my meeting. I ain't nagging. Just stating what I see, what we both see. When we have our next talk, maybe we can cover this also. I'm with you, and together we need to figure out how we want to run things."

Juan had to pause. Darlene's response wasn't the normal weak response nor the belligerent female spoiling for a fight. While her response was frank, he didn't feel she was taking a potshot at him.

"Baby, I hear ya. I get it. This is a deeper issue than it appears at first glance. Let's do sit and talk it out."

"Juan, I can do talking. Listening, as well."

"All right, baby. Listen, I gotta get back to the salt mine. I'll call you when I'm done."

"Looking forward to it. Call your girl, ya know."

"You got it. Talk to ya later."

Juan worked on the report for the next few hours. When he finished the draft report, it included a small sheath of viewgraphs and associated position papers. None of the information was particularly complicated, but it was detailed enough and located in enough different places that if a person wasn't paying close attention they might risk transposition errors. Such inconsistency would bring embarrassment to his board of directorship and his direct superior. Fortunately, in this case, Juan and his coworkers took care of business in a highly-skilled manner.

On his way home, he called Darlene like he told her he would. Her phone went straight to her voicemail. *She must be talking to one of her friends. I'll call her later,* he thought as he headed home.

Juan got home, got inside, and changed into his favorite sweats. Once he was settled, he tried to call her again. Again, it went immediately to her voicemail.

Since his girlfriend was unavailable, Juan reached in the fridge to find a bite to eat. As he scanned the fridge's contents, his cell phone rang. He checked the caller ID, and it was Darlene.

"Hey, baby. I saw you had called me a few times, so I'm calling you back. How was that work thing?"

"Ah, it was a tribute to teamwork. Nobody wanted to stay late, but to keep our jobs we sucked it up and got the task completed."

162

"There you go, baby. Rock on, why don't cha."

"How about you? How was your meeting?"

"The usual. It went fast, and I got to church in time to hear the end of Bible study."

"Oh."

"I know what you're thinking. So why didn't she answer when I called?"

"The thought had crossed my mind."

"Well, let me tell ya. There is this friend."

"Friend. A guy?"

"Yes, but nothing to worry about. You're my man. Anyway, we've known each other for a long time. I'm informally mentoring his young daughter. She's having the usual middle-school girl drama issues today, and the father called me frantically seeking advice and a woman's perspective."

Juan paused for a beat, two beats.

"Juan," Darlene asked, "you still there?"

"Yeah, I'm still here. Got a bunch of questions, though."

"Like what, exactly?"

"Like why didn't he call the girl's mom? What is she, his ex-wife? Former girlfriend? One night stand?"

"Ex-wife."

"She must not be much of a mom then if he has to call on you."

"What does that mean? Because I don't have kids, you're saying that I'm not qualified to help? The girl is struggling through school, and I know her well enough to help."

"Nah, Darlene. I don't mean you can't help. I wonder, why you? Why not some other lady? You and this guy have some history, some background that I need to know about?"

It was Darlene's turn to pause for a beat, two beats, three beats.

"Wow, my guess was right. You do have a past with this guy. Darlene, maybe you should have said something earlier."

"Say what, exactly? He doesn't mean anything to me romantically. He is not a threat to you, to what we have."

"I hear ya say that, but any time you spend with him, you're not spending it with me. Even if it's only on the phone, only if it's about his kid."

"Wow, Juan. You're jealous. I wouldn't have expected that out of you. You seem so laid back most of the time."

"Let's get this straight. I am not the guy who is gonna camp out on your doorstep to convince you to keep me over some other dude. What's his name, Bob or something?"

"Grant. His name is Grant."

"Ok, this Grant guy. What's his deal? What is he to you?"

"If you aren't sitting down, maybe you should because this could take a while." Darlene took a deep breath then proceeded telling Juan about her past relationship with Grant.

"Tough story, but it happens from time to time," Juan remarked when Darlene finished

164

the story. "But that doesn't make it right, and I still don't see why he had to call on you. He has to have other friends out there somewhere."

"Juan, I told you, Grant is a long-time friend. I couldn't just leave him hanging. And, remember, you and I weren't dating when this stuff came to a head."

"Yeah, but..."

"Juan, please let me finish. I'm trying to answer your question."

"Well, here is another. Green Valley is a pretty big church. There must have been a program to help divorced or single parents."

"Juan, I'm just about done. Please. Let me finish."

"Ok, I'm listening."

"When Helen left him, he was devastated. He had to take a couple of weeks off work to get his head together, but we all know it takes more than two weeks to get over grieving a loss like that. So, he headed back to work, could barely concentrate, and found himself struggling. The director showed uncommon grace at that time. I mean, Grant still has his job, but he's been passed over for promotion and increased opportunity. He's marking time and cashing a check, but thank God he still has a job.

As for Grace, the older Grace becomes, the mouthier she becomes. Grant has found himself wanting to beat her into submission, but thank God he called me when he got to his wit's end. He knew hitting her in the depths of

165

his anger and despair wasn't the answer. I talk to Grace from time to time, calm her down, get her to see appreciable qualities in her dad without insulting or running down her mom. I think it's bought Grant some time to try and improve his parenting skills.

Regarding your question about our church ministries, well, I wasn't a member of Green Valley at the time. At the point where Helen left, Grant didn't see a lot of resource around him. He had acquaintances, but his male friends were all happily married at the time. They didn't rally around him like perhaps they could have. I hated to see him stumble around like that."

"Darlene, I understand a little. Thanks for sharing that. But, my concern stays the same. I see that this guy could use some support. But, sooner or later he has to stand on his own two feet."

"Sounds like a typical man response. Especially coming from someone who hasn't gone through heartbreak like Grant."

"How do you know what I've gone through?"

"You're right, I don't know how much you've gone through. In time, I'm sure you'll tell me all about it. And, I will show you the same level of support if you go through it."

"Same level? I'm your boyfriend, or so you tell me. I would hope you would give more support. But, at this stage, if I go through heartbreak it would probably be caused by you."

"Probably? You think that I'm some kinda callous heartbreaker like Helen?"

"Not what I meant, Darlene. Here's my deal. This guy has gotten used to calling on you whenever he feels lonely or lost. Good thing for him. You are the right person to help, at least at the time when you didn't have a man in your life. I can see the heart and compassion you have. You are really sweet for caring that much. But now you have me in your life. I'm trying to get to know you better, wanting to spend time with you and not share you with other men. I'm concerned that this guy has gotten so used to calling on you that he'll eventually call at a time when you and I are together, having a good time, or in some deep intimate conversation. He may be in a crisis at that point. At the same moment, I may be sailing along with you, blissfully content. His crisis isn't necessarily our problem."

Darlene took in Juan's words, and the underlying sense of insecurity. She wanted to reassure him without being condescending. She struggled to come up with the right words. "Well, if nothing else, congratulations. This is our first argument. And, you seem to have stated your opinion. I don't necessarily agree with it."

"Don't necessarily agree with what? That I don't want to share you with another man? That I don't want this Grant fella in my way when I want to be with you? That you don't agree with my point of view?"

Darlene grimaced. "Juan, it isn't the end of the world if I don't agree with your point of view. Stay around me along enough. I'm sure there will be other times when we don't agree. If nothing else, your friend Dex is an easy place to disagree."

"Dex? What does Dex have to do with you and Grant?"

"You mentioned disagreeing about your point of view. I just shared another example."

"Wow, this is going in a direction I didn't expect."

"Juan, what's wrong? You knew when we met I wasn't some wallflower. I'm not some girly girl who is gonna roll over every time some pronouncement comes out of your mouth."

"Darlene, you know and I know I didn't say that. Taking a shot at Dex seems odd given the topic we were talking about."

"Look, I have an idea that may cut back on your concern. Grant and Grace get out and about once in a while. Maybe the four of us can meet somewhere soon. You can see for yourself that he isn't a threat. And as a bonus, I won't bring up your jealousy and insecurity."

"Uh, was that shot really necessary?"

"I meant nothing personal. Just stating my point of view. Just like you did."

"I know you have an independent mind. It's one of the things I like about you. I'm not trying to take away your point of view or get you to think like me. But, it's telling that as we disagreed, you found it difficult to stay on topic. Or, maybe you felt it was more fun to digress by taking a potshot at Dex. I get it. You don't like Dex. But, he really is a different topic. Sounds like you and me need to hash out where our friends rate in the midst of our relationship."

"It's not that I dislike Dex. I barely know him. But from what I have seen, he carries on like every girl-crazy man I've ever seen. No real gravity. No sense of staying power. I wouldn't dare introduce him to any friend of mine."

"You can say that without ever really sitting down and talking with him?"

"Much like your feelings about Grant, eh?"

Juan felt checkmated in this part of the conversation. If he changed topics, he thought it would appear he was running from a weak, ill-conceived viewpoint. If he stubbornly repeated his earlier words, it would appear he wasn't listening. "As we have started learning about one another, Dex hasn't in any way come between us. I will freely admit, I have seen too many cases where the woman says he's just a friend, he's no threat, then suddenly he is more than a friend and I get left holding remnants of a broken relationship. Friendship between men and women will always have that hint of something in common, something that could grow into something serious."

"Boy, Juan. You do a good job of worrying about stuff that won't happen."

"How can you say for sure it won't? I need to know for sure that if we go down this path that I think we want, that we will have every chance to make it work. I don't want Grant, Dex or anyone else getting in our way. Make sense to you?"

"Yeah. I think I get it. I understand you a little better. Must have been some sad breakups you saw and overheard."

"A couple of them, I lived through. I have no interest in willingly getting into a situation that leads to that again. I said before, I don't know what the future holds for us. Do I want to fall in love, treat you right, do the things for you to get you to stay with me for a while? Of course I do. At least, that is my intent for us as it stands now. I don't wanna spend time with you just to chase after others. I need the same from you."

Darlene exhaled audibly. "Interesting."

"What's interesting?"

"Candi said some similar things today when we were having lunch. She also mentioned that I needed to watch you, that you would show me what is important to you."

"She seems reasonable. I bet that counts for you, too."

"Juan, I think you know this, but I want to say it. I need to know that what you say now, what you promise today, has a chance of being realistic. You may change your mind tomorrow. Some little chippie may come by."

"'Chippie'?"

"Yeah, those little chicks that come around with their tight skirts and flirty attitudes. The ones that never see a guy until he has a woman with him. Then, the competition starts."

"Yeah, that reminds me. Now that you mention that, why do women do that? There are all sorts of things about women I want to find out about from you. That's one of them."

"Probably not as interesting as you might think. It's an internal grading and internal competition. Nothing more. Women want to believe their man won't cave in with some flirtatious girl when he's out with the boys. After seeing the Helen thing, I agree with you. Flirting when you are in a relationship is a recipe for disaster. If you want to flirt, flirt with your steady."

"Manoman, that sounds way too complicated."

"Juan, to us women, it really isn't that complicated. In some ways, women are closer to you guys than you realize. We have goals, just like you. We like success, just like you. Most of us aren't afraid to make tough decisions. Maybe our approach is different sometimes. That emotional roller-coaster thing can be tough. I don't always like it, but sometimes I feel like I'm riding along as a passenger in my own life. I'm thankful that God has a greater path for me than I could design for myself."

"I hear ya. I'm starting to understand how God really wants each of us to do well in serving Him. I find myself trying to understand what it is in each circumstance and sometimes find myself confusing myself."

"It happens to us all."

"Anyway, since we've seemed to cross over into the stereotype-solving discussion we planned to have, you can help me understand more about what y'all think and why."

"As a fair warning, anything we talk about in stereotype-breaking, I'll look to see if you're doing it with me."

"I know, you alluded to that earlier. I get it."

"Alright, Mister-I-get-it. We'll see."

"Look, if I didn't want to be a part of your life, I wouldn't be having this conversation with you at, wait, what time is it?"

"Wow, it's almost one o'clock in the morning. I don't know about you, but I need to get some measure of sleep. My eyes get pretty baggy and bleary if I don't get my proper rest. But, it is good talking to you and learning a little more about you."

"One thing before I go, though. I wanna let you know I really, really like hearing you talk. I'm looking forward to hearing what else comes out of your mouth."

"I hope you still feel that way next time we disagree. You may get tired of my mouth if we don't see eye to eye down the road."

"Good point, Darlene. Anyway, I'll let you go for now. Don't want to, but I will."

"Juan, you are sweet. I look forward to hearing your voice a little more too. How about tomorrow? Game a call?"

"You know it, sweetheart. Pleasant dreams."
"You too, baby. Night night."

CHAPTER 28

Juan got up early the next day. With a big meeting fairly early in the schedule, he made a point of getting all his resources together.

As he started making copies of the presentation charts, he thought back to his conversation with Darlene. He envisioned more conversations to come. Quiet, peaceful times where they could get down to the deep, nitty-gritty ideas that would help them understand one another better. He had encountered women before, even in casual conversations, who enjoyed being enigmas. It was frustrating for him to want to have a real conversation but not being able to get past the crusty level of wordsmithing and indirect verbiage. It was refreshing and addicting having Darlene in his life. He enjoyed their back and forth banter without it being personal attacks or putdowns.

As he gathered his sets of charts for stapling, Juan looked at a clock on the wall. Time had zoomed by and it was after twelve o'clock noon. The meeting was another forty-five minutes away, enough time to send Darlene a quick e-mail. Nothing earth-shattering. No big revelations. Just a guy telling his girl he was thinking of her.

A few minutes later, he worked his way to the main conference room.

The executive secretary came out of the conference room to make the 10-minutes prior call to get the attendees seated. The group responded cattle-like to their respective chairs.

Juan sat directly behind his boss in order to provide a quick response to any possible questions in his area of expertise.

The meeting went by smoothly and rather quickly. His boss was well pleased.

"Between you, Julia, and Mac, you all did an outstanding job with this effort," his boss complimented. "Since you all stayed late last night, I'm giving the three of you the rest of the afternoon and tomorrow off. You've earned it."

"Yes, sir," Juan responded. "I appreciate it, as we all do. Thank you very much."

Immediately, he went to his office, picked up the phone, and called Darlene.

"Hello, Darlene. It's Juan." He used his cold, telephone-professional voice, which he realized was out of place when talking to his girl.

"Hi, Juan. This is Darlene," she mimicked, using the same solemn intonation he used in his greeting. "What's up with you, sweetie? You sound a little grim. Did your meeting not go well? I know you put in a lot of effort getting ready."

"Aw, honey. I'm just messing with you. Actually, all is well. Actually very well. Guess what?"

"What?"

"Seems my boss was so happy with our working late nights and long hours getting ready for the meeting that he gave us the rest of today and all of Friday off. I'm tightening up stuff in the office before leaving. I got an idea. Can I bring you lunch?"

"Wow, congrats on the time off. And yes, I'm hungry. I have a taste for shrimp lo mein. How about you?"

"I'll be there in about half an hour. See ya then."

"Bring it on, sweetie. Looking forward to lunching with you."

Once Juan completed his closeout actions, he headed towards a nearby Chinese restaurant. He pulled up, entered, placed his order and waited for his food.

The order was completed, the bill was paid, and Juan took his lunch to his girlfriend. He got to the newspaper building, and once inside encountered a stern-looking receptionist.

"How may I help you, sir?"

"Hello, I'm Juan Smith. I'm here to see Darlene Jones."

"Yes sir. I was told to expect you. Here." She handed Juan a visitor's badge. "Go up to the fifth floor, turn left and her office is third door on your right, office number 511. Have a nice day."

"Thank you, ma'am." Juan clipped the visitor's badge to his necktie, grabbed his food, and headed to a bank of elevators off to one side.

As he got off the elevator on the fifth floor, he took a quick look around to see what else was listed on the fifth floor. Eventually, he made that left turn, headed down the hallway, and found office number 511. The door was slightly ajar. He knocked softly, three gentle taps. He heard a whispered, "Come in."

Darlene was finishing up a teleconference. She nodded towards a small oval table for Juan to rest the takeout food. He did so, then took a seat.

"We'll talk later. Take care. Bye." Darlene hung up her phone, and shook her head softly.

"Sounds like an interesting debate. Otherwise, how you doing, baby?"

"I'm good. Gonna be better in about five minutes or so when I get some food in my system."

"Glad to do it."

Juan reached in the bag and brought out two takeout containers, napkins, and two packs of chopsticks. "Hope this turns out good, Darlene. I've used this restaurant many times, but I always get broccoli beef. Don't know how the lo mein is gonna turn out. If it isn't good, please let me know and we can try something else next time."

"Baby, don't worry. It's gonna be good. Haven't had lo mein in forever. Yum-my. Say grace for us, please."

Juan asked God's blessing over the food, then the couple dug in. Darlene wielded her chopsticks with an uncommon grace.

"Is there anything you aren't good at? You handle those sticks like you were raised in the Far East," Juan said.

"Man, lemme tell ya. It's all just practice. Saw it done on a movie once, thought it looked

177

interesting, tried it that night. Got spaghetti all over my clothes the first time and got eggs and bacon all over my school clothes the next morning." Darlene laughed. "But, I stayed with it until I got it right. Kids at school thought I was nuts, but I was determined to see that thing through to the end."

"Impressive. Were you always that way, seeing things through to the end?"

"You know it. No sense trying if you aren't gonna see it to the conclusion. Don't get me wrong, some things I started were a mistake from the start. I certainly didn't see those through completion, like playing youth league football as an eight year old."

"You played football as a kid?"

"Of course, didn't everyone?"

"Not every girl."

"Every girl didn't have hands like mine. I never dropped a pass."

"Never? C'mon. You must be kidding. Everyone drops a pass." Juan was highly impressed. He took a bit of his food and chuckled.

"Juan, hear me. I was the best receiver in the league. And, I never, repeat never, dropped a pass in a game or practice. It got to the point where boys didn't want to cover me 'cause I would embarrass them. Too bad puberty hit. I quit growing, and the boys got bigger and faster. But, I can still run a square-out pattern as well as anyone my age."

"The more I listen to you, the more I find out, the more I get pulled in."

"I can't help it that I'm amazing," she said jokingly. "I'm only what God made me to be. I'm kidding on the amazing comment, I hope you know. You are pretty much good-to-go as well. Congrats again on the successful presentation this morning. I guess your boss was relieved and overjoyed."

"Well, of course I didn't do it alone. My coworkers know their stuff, and aren't afraid to share info. The prep was long, but pleasant. Julia, our viewgraph expert, composes viewgraphs that get to the point. They're also so striking, they could almost be fine art. And Bob McKenzie, our resident engineering expert, can look at a proposal or requirements document and see flaws, hidden costs and unintended consequences better than anyone in the city. When I work with them, I can't help but smile. They are the best, and know how to really break it down. They make me look smart, and they don't feel that they are being taken advantage of. I love being a part of the team."

"Juan, it shows. Good on ya, love."

"Enough about work. What's up for you tonight? You wanna get together and talk a bit?"

"Tonight isn't good. Homework for me, prepping a column and getting ready for next week's call-in. But, I have time this weekend. Let me finish stuff today and tonight, so my Friday is flexible. Sound good to you?"

"Yeah, baby. You've got a date."

"Alright. I can't wait."

Lunch with Juan was pleasant. The food was light and tasty, and hanging out with him was fun. The light-hearted banter had her laughing out loud at several of his comments and observations. She was starting to learn that he had a great, quirky sense of humor. Darlene was really getting a sense of relaxation with him. He appeared to be a great guy the more she got to know him.

As they finished the meal, Juan got up and cleaned up the containers and other food material.

"Thanks, baby," Darlene whispered as she kissed him on the cheek. She noticed he neither flinched nor forced an awkward bit of PDA. He touched her lightly on her shoulder and his hand felt warm on that spot. She felt relieved he didn't feel compelled to grab her in a vulgar fashion in her office. His acting relaxed in turn relaxed her.

"I know what you're thinking, Darlene."

"What are you talking about? What am I thinking?"

"You're relieved I didn't embarrass you by groping you here. Trust me, babe. One, we agreed to be chaste. No sense inflaming each other by grabbing body parts in the workplace. Two, there is a level of professionalism required in your office, my office, or any other work environment." He walked over to a plastic dispenser on the wall and wiped his hands with some antibacterial liquid. "I know it's time for you to get back at it. I had a blast doing this with you. Let's do it again soon. You pick the food, I bring it in. All right?"

"All right, man. Thanks again. I feel *gooood*," Darlene crooned as she rubbed her belly.

"I'm out. See ya later, honey."

"See *you* later, baby. Again, thanks for lunch."

Juan smiled, nodded, gave Darlene one more gentle hug, and left her office. She sat down at her desk fairly glowing. She had such a sense of peace about Juan. It really felt like the best was yet to come. She was in a great mood the rest of the day.

Recovering from the reverie, she hit the last tasks and information gathering with renewed vigor. Before long, it was time to go home. She shut down the office, took the elevator down the stairs, headed to the car, popped the top on her convertible and away she sped. *This day was one of the best ever,* she thought. *God is truly kind and gracious.*

CHAPTER 29

Nine o'clock in the evening, and Darlene's phone rang. Her ring tone was a classical snippet, something that reminded her of peaceful times. "Hello?"

"Hey, how are you doing?"

"I was just thinking about you. Real good thoughts. My housework is done, the stuff I brought from the office is cleared, and I'm all yours this evening. You like?"

"Mmmm, I like." Hearing Darlene say she was thinking about him raised Juan's ego a couple of notches. "So, tell me, what kinda housekeeping were you doing?"

"Ugh, the bathroom. I hate it, but it's gotta be done. I especially hate the smell of cleaner on my hands, and I end up washing them several times when I'm done."

"I hear ya. I hate that too. I love it when the bathroom is sparkling, but I hate the stuff I gotta go through to get there. Been cleaning bathrooms since I was a boy, and it doesn't get any more enjoyable."

"I can relate. Hey, I just noticed that this is one of the few things you've mentioned about your childhood. There is so much about your past I don't know, so much about you that I don't know. I wanna hear more and you have my complete attention. How do I know you aren't some kind of killer or something?"

"Yeah, how do you know?" Juan chuckled. After a pause, he cleared his throat for dramatic effect. "Ok, I'll open up about lots of stuff but you gotta do the same, at least as long as we can stand being on the phone."

"No problem, can do. I'm seated and ready. Go," she said.

"Well, first off I was born here in town. I'm an only child. Parents were born here too, and they've been together since they were small kids. I guess you can say they've pretty much been a couple all their lives."

"Oh, really?"

"It gets even stranger. They were born within three weeks of each other and were backyard neighbors as kids."

"Wow, what are the odds? Uncommon, even."

"I know. Their families knew one another, and each of them grew in a similar environment. Same mindset, same economic background, parents thought the same way. They were around each other so much that they always expected to be in each other's lives. They rarely had days where they weren't in the same schools, same college, same social circles."

"How about church? Were your parents active in church?"

"Somewhat. I don't remember either of them leading ministry efforts, but if someone from church called needing help, they would pitch in. On Sundays, they made sure we were in church. We sat together on the pew, sang along with the songs, listened to the sermon and went home."

"Not trying to pick, but did you feel that was enough?"

"Well, as a kid I never thought about it. Maybe I took it for granted that it would come eventually. When we got home after church, my folks would talk about stuff, but nothing too spiritually deep or enlightening. It was normally who was wearing what, who didn't speak to whom, how the choir sounded on a particular song or what they thought about the sermon. I guess now I get it, we weren't as involved as we could have been."

"How about now? Your parents more involved?"

"My mom is. She does some Sunday School teaching, helps out with mentoring. My dad? I think he drives my mom to the church."

Darlene laughed a bit. "Well, growth comes different for everyone. God gives opportunities, but it's up to us to take advantage."

Juan felt slightly uncomfortable at the sense that Darlene was grading him on his past. "How 'bout your parents, and your background?"

"My parents were pretty cool. I think you would have really liked them."

"Would have liked them?" repeated Juan.

"Yeah, they've been deceased for a few years now."

"Oh. I didn't know. I'm sorry."

"It's ok. I know in the end they're in heaven with God. They were saved and died in His service."

"What happened to them, if you don't mind me asking?"

"They were missionaries. God put it on my dad's heart in his youth to spread the Gospel abroad. They did stints in the Caribbean, rural Canada, parts of Africa. A couple of times, when I was out of school for the summer, they took me with them. I learned a lot about people, about God, and about my parents during those times. Watching them work, watching them pray over people. Wow." Darlene paused, not to cry but to savor the memories.

"That had to be such an uplift."

"You know it. Anyway, on their last mission, my mom got sick, real sick with a highly contagious disease. My dad, bless his soul, wouldn't leave my her side, regardless of how virulent the disease. He did all he could to make her comfortable. She died on a Monday. He had been fighting it, too so he could help take care and comfort her in the end. After she passed, he wrote me a note and forwarded it through mission channels. A week later, he was gone on to his heavenly reward as well. I had just turned nineteen when I got the news. I thought they would be home in another month or so. In a fashion, they were. We had their funerals as one service, about a week and a half after their remains got back to the States."

Juan was speechless. Just imagining what she'd been through, he started to realize a powerful level of depth in Darlene. "Wow, I had no idea."

"I was cool with it and still am. How many people actually give their lives in service to the Lord? They did it. They actually did it. No, they were not perfect. My dad could be very forgetful, and my mom laughed at her jokes before anybody else got the chance to decide if the jokes were actually funny. That got to the point where it sometimes drove me crazy. But, they fit together. The way God made the two of them, they fit like puzzle pieces. Individually, they loved God first. Because of whom He made them to be, they learned to love one another. All the best clichés you've heard about what romantic love could be, they lived almost all of 'em. If I ever get married, and my marriage is half as solid and committed as theirs was, I'll be good to go. My husband-to-be has a lot to live up to, but I will be beside him every step of the way. Every step."

Juan was speechless yet again. Darlene had a level of expression that was exhilarating and scary at the same time. He wanted a woman in his life who had her sense of clarity, but he frankly didn't know if he was man enough to match it.

"You're quiet. What's up in your head?"

"Just thinking. You've been through a lot," Juan said, sounding somewhat gloomy.

"No more than any other person. I thank God for seeing me through it all. Hey, since this is starting to sound heavy, let's lighten the mood. What's your favorite color?"

"Black, but I know some folk say black is a shade, not a color. Whatever, I like it as a color. And you?"

"Blue violet, purple or whatever you call it. I like darker colors more than the lighter ones. I know it's not girlish, me not liking pink or yellow or lavender. Rich, dark colors give me a sense of calm, deep quiet, like looking at the ocean at sundown. They look good on most fabrics, too, in my opinion. Ok, now your turn. Ask me something. Don't be shy, man. Bring it on."

"Okay. What's your favorite Sunday meal?"

"When I was a kid, my mom made the best macaroni and cheese from scratch. A little flour in the cheese sauce for thickening, cooking it in the oven long enough for that bit of brown crusting on top. That, along with her roast chicken, dark meat of course, and collard greens. With all that work, she would cook it on Saturday, then warm it up after church on Sunday. The temptation to sneak a taste drove me crazy. Once she caught me, whipped my butt good. Didn't do that again." Darlene laughed.

"Mmm, sounds yummy. Your mom must have been a good cook."

"Yeah, she was."

"For me, pork chops, cabbage, corn bread and a slice of sweet potato pie hits the spot. My mom and my dad were both good cooks, and they took turns each week. My dad liked cooking inside, since he would be near the television to watch his favorite old movies while he cooked. My mom loved grilling, and would grill anything, any time of year. Meats, fish, veggies. We used to joke that she would grill desserts on New Year's Day if no one was looking."

"Do you cook like either of them? You got skills in the kitchen?"

"Nah, I don't take nearly the time they did to learn or prep. Guess I don't have the patience."

"Well, sir, patience is something God specializes in. Stick with me, and I'll have you cooking all kinds of stuff, and we'll take our time. Definitely take our time. Now, my turn again. This one is a tough one, so don't take it personally. Your buddy, Dex, how long have the two of you been friends?"

"Since grade school. We both played youth league basketball, both played two-guard. He started; I was his backup. Lots of times in practice, he was the guy who could keep everybody loose, cracking jokes and being silly. He was a pretty good ball player, but as you see neither one of us is very tall. Ball stopped being fun when we stopped growing. We stayed friends, though."

"I see. Makes sense."

"I guess you're probably curious to know about him because of his attitude, his way of dealing with women."

"And you are absolutely correct," Darlene replied.

"Well, let me tell you a little about Dex, then maybe his attitude will make more sense to you. In our junior year of high school, he fell head-over-heels for a girl in our algebra class. He bought into the hype, the "anything you want, baby girl" mentality. We saw it in sitcoms, we heard it in songs, we saw it in advice columns. He tried it. He sacrificed for her, gave her every trinket he could. The girl, once she got to know Dex, felt she could do better. She felt she could find a guy with bigger muscles or a better car. She dumped him during lunch in the cafeteria one Friday. No set-up, no *let 'em down easy,* no *we can still be friends* even. She just walked up to him while he was in the middle of chowing down his tater tots and broke the news to him. I'll never forget the look on his face. He was completely astonished and unprepared. To his credit, he didn't break down in public. But, after about a week or so of grief, he resolved to never let another female get close enough to him to hurt him in that way. He figured he'd get them before they could get to him."

"Sounds rough, Juan. How do you feel about that? You agree with his approach?"

"I don't agree with how he responded, but I see his point somewhat. The girl in question didn't give him any prior inkling that she was

189

looking at going in a different direction. She strung him along, accepted the gifts and attention, and no sooner than he relaxed and thought she was gonna stay around a while, she left him hanging. Even some of her friends admitted later that they didn't agree with the manner she used."

"So, does that leave you as a man who distrusts women, like Dex?"

"No," Juan blurted. He caught himself and had to admit, "Well, maybe a bit, I guess. I try to keep my eyes open. I want to share, want to be concerned and compassionate. I want the lady – want *you* to know and see me as sincere and trustworthy. However, I don't wanna get burned either. Now it's your turn."

"Okay, what's your question?"

"Why do girls do that to guys? You know you want us to pursue you. You allow us to chase when there really is no hope in our catching up."

Now it was Darlene's time to catch herself. She wanted to blurt out some emotional, passionate explanation. She also suspected Juan wouldn't understand that emotional view. After all, he was a man.

"I can't speak for every woman, but for me and I have a bit of an explanation. Ultimately, it's insecurity, whether we're dealing with a guy or dealing with other women. No matter who we think we are, for many women there's that nagging voice in our heads that says we aren't good enough, not smart enough, nowhere near pretty enough. No matter how many self-affirming books we read, or how many shows on television we watch to remind us to love ourselves, the clothes that are supposed to make us feel desirable, we still struggle with the question of are we good enough. I know that God didn't make us to live insecure lives. It isn't Godly, but it really grips some of us. It also makes us wonder if we're making the right decisions, spending time in the right ways or with the right people. Many of us second guess ourselves on almost everything."

"I suspected as much."

"Oh, really?" Darlene responded, with a hint of skepticism. "Like the man on late-night television says, 'But wait, there's more!' It feeds the love-hate relationships we have with men, in large part because we struggle to have healthy, supportive friendships with women. No matter how close or how long we befriend another female, there is always a risk that some small issue will scrape up against our insecurity, convince us that someone doesn't accept or approve us as who we are, and deny us the outlet to deal with it. I really envy men in this area."

"Because our friendships aren't as intense? Because our friendships seem so shallow?" Juan's attempt at humor failed dismally.

Darlene paused for a beat, just to rub it in. "I wouldn't say less intense or shallow. Men have a way of accepting each other, at least when you actually make the effort. No matter what age, even. At a distance, I've seen boys in the playground, guys in the gym when I was in college, or even old dudes under a shady tree in the park playing chess or checkers. The one thing common in all situations was an atmosphere of acceptance. Of course, I wasn't close enough to hear everything being said. But, as they were having fun, it looked like they were all in the moment. The enjoyment then was enough. There was no insecurity about who was wearing what, no hidden intent when something was said, or even if something wasn't said but should have been said."

"Yeesh, how complicated. Don't know if I ever even thought about stuff like that in the midst of a game. Too busy trying to win, I guess. And, before you say it, I know winning on the sandlot isn't everything. I understand that in the bigger picture, it didn't mean much. But it was fun to try, fun to compete against someone who was trying the same thing at the same time."

"As you would say, that explains a lot. As women, sometimes our insecurities can get in the way of what we can do. So often it takes us until middle age or later to finally reach that place of inner acceptance. So much fellowship and mutual support we willingly give away, just because we can't get past ourselves." Darlene took a deep breath, and sighed. "That's enough about that."

Juan found himself mulling over what his new girlfriend described. He wanted to be blunt, but didn't want to put a wedge in their relationship so early. He quickly mulled over a couple of possible responses.

"There you go, being quiet again. What's on your mind now?"

"Just thinking about you. In so many ways, really in every way, you're different from every woman I've ever met. I like that. I really do."

"That's sweet. I like you too."

"Actually, Darlene, I'd like to go further with this, with us. Maybe something long-term."

Darlene gasped. She could sense that Juan might have taken that the wrong way, so she quickly responded, "Well, that's certainly possible."

"So we both understand, I mean like the journey of our life together. Learning about one another. Growing close. Becoming a team. Haven't done it much, but I really think we can make a go of this thing. I'm excited about it. You?"

"Well, yeah. Maybe you're right."

Darlene took a deep breath, then asked, "Juan, can I get a favor from you? I know it's short notice, but I want to ask before we get much further."

"Yeah, ask away."

"Would you mind praying for us from time to time? I'm not trying to put you on the spot, and I'm not demanding you pray for us every night, but I hope the Holy Spirit leads you to do it. Are you uncomfortable with that?" Darlene asked, with sincerity resonating in her voice.

"Sure, no problem," Juan answered quickly. He didn't actually think it over, but felt it was just a function of his willingness to commit.

CHAPTER 30

When Darlene's alarm went off, without grumbling she slowly opened her eyes, yawning at the same time. After all, it was Friday, seven o'clock, and she had nothing scheduled on her calendar. She turned off the alarm, rotated to where she could sit up on the edge of the bed, and thanked God for a restful night's sleep. She also prayed for Juan. "Lord, please guide Juan today. Make your direction in his life so clear that he can't miss what you're trying to do and say to him."

She found herself surprisingly chipper and almost girlish. Darlene hadn't felt this carefree for this long in a while. She had been content, knowing her relationship with the Lord was good and getting better. But, she felt a giddiness that surprised her. Just as she noticed the change in her demeanor, her smart phone buzzed. She checked, and saw she had a text from Juan:

"Good morning, sweetheart. Have a great day."

She felt a smile spread across her face. He was thinking of her at that moment. Maybe he was the kind of responsive guy who, with a little shaping, could be a stand-up, believer boyfriend.

She grabbed her phone and started a return text. "Good morning to you too. I hope to see ya later."

As Darlene hit SEND, she swiveled in her chair to face the computer screen. Opening up browsers, e-mail applications and documents, she got herself ready for another day.

Friday in the office flowed free and easy. Meetings were brisk and to the point. She shared ideas about future columns that were met with nearly universal support. She kept up with the issues of the day with ease, while thoughts of Juan crept in easily.

As she plowed through the afternoon's research, the thought of spending time with her beau was a pleasant distraction. *What about lunch outside tomorrow?* she wondered. *I bet he'd get a kick out of it.* After a quick check of the weather forecast (partly cloudy, with a high in the upper 50s), she sent him a short e-mail.

`"How about lunch in the park tomorrow?"`

Scant seconds passed, then a one-word e-mail response popped up in her browser: `"Yes!"`

She started composing a response when her office phone rang. "Hello."

"I'm all in," Juan said as soon as Darlene answered. "I'll chill some water and juice tonight, come get you mid-morning or so. Any particular juice you want?"

"As long as it's not grapefruit juice, otherwise water is always good. I'm looking forward to spending some quiet time with you."

"Yeah, I feel the same way. We don't get outside and play nearly enough. I know I could use some playtime. Office work is important, but it can get repetitive. I miss the sun."

"Cool, then. What about picking me up tomorrow around eleven? Is that good for you?"

"Yeah, that sounds good. It'll be good to hang with you for the day. Till then, have a great finish at work. I'll call you tonight."

"Talk to you later, baby."

CHAPTER 31

"Oooooh, a picnic. Isn't that romantic? Bro, this Darlene chick is changing you, man."

"Dex, shouldn't that be the case? Shouldn't we be looking for something different when a man finds a woman? Anyway, this is a good next step. We can spend the day talking, finding out more about one another."

"You are such a square. Talk, talk, talk. Any other hundred guys would be trying to get her somewhere quiet and dark, and do...you know..."

"Yeah, yeah. I hear you, but we've gone over this before. I want to impress her, give this thing every opportunity to work out. And, I've also told you if things don't work, I don't want some lingering emotional mess getting in the way. If it's gonna end, I want the break to be clean with as few entanglements as possible."

"Hit it and quit it, eh?"

"I'm not 'hitting' anything. She deserves better, and actually so do I. I'm tired of the same old mess. The misunderstandings. Disrespect. Threats. Breakups with tears and throwing stuff. Nah, I'm done with all that. And actually, there's one more thing."

"What's that?"

"What if we've been wrong all these years? God has given us directions, how to deal with women, and we've ignored it. There are so many people who are either in bad relationships or who've left failed ones. So many are walking the streets not trusting each other emotionally. You meet a girl, and the second thing you think is how is the situation gonna end."

"Oh, yeah? What's the first thing? Oh, never mind. We all know the first thing. Or, I should say most of us know what that first thing is." Dex chuckled at his observation, as he usually did. " I see now enlightened guys like you today see things clearer than real street brothas like me."

"See, that ain't it at all. It's been hitting me hard lately. None of our hands are clean when it comes to how we deal with women. And, you could say none of their hands are clean when they deal with us."

"Man, you analyze stuff way too much."

"Dex, generations of us haven't thought about it hard enough. Think about it; there are so many frustrated and angry women out here. How does that bear out in the long run?"

"I don't know. Angry babies? Angry pets?"

"In a way, yeah. You meet women at the club every month, right?"

"Yeah, you know me, bro. No problem meeting 'em."

"Yeah, but what happens after you meet 'em? What are you always telling me? This one don't have any common sense. That one is always complaining."

"That's just the way of the world today. If you wanna get some lemonade, you got to put up with the bitter taste of the lemon. All you gotta do is squeeze 'em a little, pour some sugar in the juice, and *aaaah*, so refreshing."

Juan laughed a bit at Dex's silliness. "Yeah, I get it. But, one lemon can only make so much juice. What I'm talking about is much more widespread than the one girl you meet. You go out, you hear women saying, 'He can't do nothing for me but pay my bills.' They're all holding out for some kind of perfect knight that doesn't even exist. It's similar to us holding out for the perfect girl when none are out there. We are all broken. We do so much damage to ourselves and one another, then we're stunned when relationships fail.

Dex didn't have a quip for this point.

"Dex, you remember Dolores Robinson from seventh grade?"

"Yeah, I do. She was cute. She was a cheerleader, ran track, played softball."

"Well, I hurt that girl so bad. She had a crush on me, but I never gave her the time of day. Dunno why, because she was cool. Have no idea what I was thinking. I could've at least been civil. Maybe that would have kept the door open for the future."

"I just saw her downtown a few months ago, out with some friends at a happy hour. She was looking good. What was wrong with her?"

"Absolutely nothing, which is part of my point. It's okay if we aren't attracted to this lady or that. But, how do we handle it? When a girl isn't attracted to a guy, she can shoot him down, no harm no foul. We're expected to move along. But when we say not to a girl, she gets consumed with self-doubt. Or, she rebounds with an angry version of all men are dogs. So now, you come along, but since she's still mad at me, she doesn't want you near her. This goes back to Darlene. This time, I don't want any kind of regret or remorse. I want to make sure she sees the real me in every action, every statement. No misunderstanding. No regret."

"You gotta be kidding. You're putting way too much thought into this. You're trying too hard, taking it too seriously. You gotta ease into this thing."

"Ease into it? Look who's talking mister-hit-it-and-quit-it."

"Yeah, you heard me. You know me, I'm gonna be me regardless. But you, you always were a different type of guy. I guess I shouldn't be too surprised over your idea about this." Dex took a couple of deep breaths. " Have you talked to your girl about the way you see it?"

"A little bit."

"You think she's gone through similar? She doesn't seem all that angry or high-strung to me."

"I don't get a sense of it in her spirit. About us, she seems mellow but enthusiastic, if that makes any sense. I don't know what her buttons are, what makes her angry."

"Women being women, you'll find out soon enough. You still gonna hit the gym before your date?"

"Of course. Just 'cause I'm dating doesn't mean all my life has changed. I still need to hit the gym, still need that workout time."

"Yeah, you gotta stay ripped, 'cause you know the lady will lose interest if you lose that edge. In other news, what's going on with that man who you said was interested in your girl?"

"His name is Grant. She hasn't said anything about him lately."

"Darlene is an attractive woman. This Grant guy no doubt knows the same. I bet if you were out of the picture, he would love to make a cozy home with his daughter and your woman. You better keep a watch on him."

"You're just seeing things."

"Keep watching, is all I've got to say about it," Dex answered.

"'Preciate your concern, but I got this. And if he tries to get a little closer or get in the way somewhat, I'll deal with him. I guess he sees that Darlene and I are starting something, and there isn't room for some other dude hanging around."

"I understand your words, but remember he was her friend long before you two met. Whether or not you like it, he's a part of her life. Here you come along, and you fit in her life in some ways. I predict he will have a crisis, and probably soon. Something that only she can do for him. Something that, if she does that, will take away from your time with her. Then, the question will come up about your jealousy and insecurity. It sounds like a no-win to me. If you don't show any concern, then the lady thinks you don't care enough about people in general. You're a cold-hearted man. If you act jealous and possessive, that scares the lady into thinking you're some irrational guy driven by emotion and temper. You're getting ready to face some trials in this thing, and my suggestion is you better think about those things before they come up. If you try to deal with it on the fly, you may or may not come up with the right answer."

Juan couldn't help but pause. As much as he usually disregarded Dex's inputs regarding romance and relationships, this time there were some nuggets of truth. He sensed that these nuggets would rear their ugly heads.

Oh, and one more thing. Now that you've signed up for this girl, you gotta realize that everything you do around her, for her, or with her, gets graded."

"What do you mean by graded?"

"C'mon, man. You know. You been around. Whatever you say will get filtered. Whatever you buy for her will be assessed based on how much you listen to what she says. Everything you do will become a part of how she sees you. Everything you do will be a reflection of how you see her and value her. Everything now will require some sort of reaction or response. And, your reaction or response better be quick. Women hate procrastinating men."

"I get it. I really do. But I don't think it's gonna be like that with Darlene. I know it's happening all around us, but she isn't like that. Trust me, I know."

"Yeah, you know all right. Don't forget, I've been the guy who listened when you vented about this girl or that. Some of this is gonna come back to you, real quick. Keep your head up."

CHAPTER 32

Saturday morning started mostly cloudy with threatening skies. Not what young lovers would want on an outing to a park, but Juan was determined to make the best of it. After all, he had love alongside his life, and even a rainy day had potential. *Looks like the weatherman got it wrong,* Juan observed. *Better take a jacket and come up with a backup plan.* He grabbed his cell phone and called Darlene. "Hello, sweetie cakes."

"Good morning to you. How are you?"

"I'm well. Have you looked outside this morning?" asked Juan.

"Yeah, I see there are more clouds than we expected. But, it's still a fine day, and I still wanna go for it. If it rains, we can go to plan B. You agree?"

"I'm with you, honey. I'm on the way. I'll be there in a couple of hours."

"Okay. Bye."

No sooner than Darlene hung up, the phone rang again. It was Grant.

"Hey, Darlene. How are things today?"

"I'm good. How are you and Grace? Is she alright?"

"I'm worried," Grant confessed. "I can't shake this feeling that something is going on in her head, but she won't tell me. I don't know if it's some boy or something else. I'm worried, because I just can't seem to get through to her. You got a few minutes?"

"Well, actually no. My boyfriend is coming by soon to pick me up."

Grant paused, searching for something to say. "I hope he's a cool dude. Does he treat you well?"

"Yeah, so far he's been every bit the gentleman. I like him."

"Do you really?"

"Yeah, I do. Don't know what the future holds, but we're gonna go down this road for a bit, see what we see, and go from there."

Grant paused again, then followed with, "Well, as long as he treats you good. If he gets out of line, though, gimme a call and we'll straighten him out with the quickness." With that, Grant said his goodbye and hung up.

No sooner did she hang up from Grant, Darlene's phone rang yet again.

"Good morning, Darlene. God bless you. How are you?" Carli asked.

"I'm doing great, Carli. Just getting ready to go hang out with my man for a bit. The weather looks a bit dicey, but we'll make a go of it. What's going on with you today?"

"Not much, hon. Just hadn't heard from you in a few days, so I called to check in on you. You sound like you're on top of the world. Just a little bit giddy, I guess."

"Giddy, maybe. Carli, you know me better than anyone. I don't normally gush about anybody, but Juan is a good man. I really think the more time we spend together, and the more we get to know one another, we might see that we really have something."

"I know he seems to have a lot of good qualities, but still, take it slow. That's all I'll offer. Just like before with Grant. You took it slow, and because of all the stuff he has going on, going slow was the right thing to do."

"Speaking of Grant, he called me right before you did. Do you know what's going on with Grace?"

"No, I don't talk with him as much as before. A wave in passing is about as good as it gets. What's up with Grace? She in some kind of trouble?"

"I'm not sure. We didn't talk long."

"Hmm. Not like Grant. Normally, he can be pretty talkative. What did you say to him?"

"What do you mean? I wasn't insulting."

"Darlene, c'mon. You've known Grant for how many years? You know how he adores you, turns to you whenever he needs a friendly ear. If he knows about Juan it probably rocked him to the core. You were part of his reality, someone he could count on anytime. Now, to him you've ran off with some other guy the same way Helen ran off. And, Juan probably senses that as well. Sometime soon, he's probably going to bring up Grant's presence, if not his name. On some level, Grant loves you. At least, that's my guess."

Darlene heard the chime, followed by a light knock. "Carli, can you hold a bit? I think Juan is at the door." Darlene opened the door and smiled as she saw Juan standing on her stoop.

"Come on in. Make yourself at home. I'm on the phone, but I'll be done in a sec."

Juan entered and kissed Darlene sweetly on her cheek. He took a seat on the leather couch in the living room.

"Well, Carli, Juan is here. I gotta run."

"Okay. You two have a good time."

"Thanks. We'll definitely catch up at church. Bye."

Juan took Darlene's hand and spun her around, as if they were ballroom dancing. "You are such a beautiful lady. Being with you is fun and easy."

"Fun? Yea. Easy? We'll see. Hey, can you help me with the cooler?"

"Sure, darling. Let's load up and get out of here."

Darlene spun out of Juan's embrace and walked towards her kitchen. She had a cooler and a basket set up and ready to go.

The couple walked to Juan's car, with Darlene lacing her arm into the crook of Juan's as he carried the picnic supplies. A quick load-in, and they were off.

The drive to the park and wildlife reserve was scenic, with numerous switchbacks and winding curves. The sun peeked through dense, grey clouds, and scattered streaks of sunlight slid to the ground.

Darlene stared out of the window, taking in the scenery as it sped by. "Juan, what kind of music do you like?"

"I'm not a huge music fan. I use it more as background, since I don't like absolute quiet. My folks were big Al Green fans and my dad loved Jerry Lee Lewis."

"Jerry Lee Lewis, eh? Well, I've had exposure to classical and gospel is always good for my spirit. That reminds me, I gotta share with you this choir I heard last year. Excuse me. My phone is buzzing."

Darlene reached in her phone and checked her caller ID. It was Grant again.

"Hi, Grant. Yeah, I'm busy." Darlene glanced at Juan, who returned her glance with a begrudging nod. "Grace said what? Of course, yeah. I know she has her ups and downs...she said what? Well, look, can I call you back a little later when I get home?"

Juan noticed the time on his car's dashboard. Her conversation had only been a couple of minutes, but he felt it was infringing on precious time he wanted with his lady. This Grant guy, regardless of the reason, was blocking. Juan didn't like it at all. *If it ain't suicide, she needs to let him go,* Juan thought.

"Okay," Darlene went on. "Have her call me tonight. Take care. Goodbye."

"Seems like dude has issues with being a father to his kid. What's the deal now?"

"He wouldn't give me all the details, but sounds like a typical kid upset. He said something about grounding her. She rebelled a bit. He's trying not to let emotion and temper get the better of him."

"He oughtta beat that butt for a while. A couple of swats on the behind will straighten her out."

"I can't believe you said that," Darlene exclaimed. "A little harsh, don't you think?"

"Harsh? I don't know about that. To me, it seems obvious. Who's the father over there, and who's the child? Sounds like she's forgotten her role, and it may be that she's just a little spoiled."

"Maybe to you, but you don't know what that child has gone through. The abandonment issues, not to mention adolescence, body changes, puberty, self-image issues. She has a lot going on in her head, and guys aren't always wired to understand what a girl endures."

"See, I disagree with that. Maybe I don't have sisters or a daughter, but it seems like most of this stuff isn't some new revelation. People have been going through this stuff for generations. All kinds of research can inform any man how to deal with raising a daughter."

"You raise crops, but you rear children. She's not a rutabaga. She's a troubled young girl who needs stability in her life."

"Maybe, but are you the one to do it?"

"Girls her age crave role models. I'm honored that she chose me. And one more thing. There is more to child rearing than book knowledge. Every child is different. Books can't cover every eventuality, every bit of heartbreak or confusion. She needs a human connection."

Juan had to take a breath. Their conversation was getting a bit deep. He noted Darlene's passionate tone. He was turned on by her passion for something she cared about, but he was frustrated that it took a few moments away from the lovey-dovey stuff he wanted from his lady.

"You make good points, Darlene. I'm not in Grant's shoes and I don't know what he's going through, but I will say that he's fortunate to have a friend like you."

"You're kind and wise. I knew there was a reason I like you so much." Darlene clasped Juan's right hand in hers. "I'm glad you see things my way," she kidded.

Juan put on a mock scowl, but couldn't hold back a sly smile.

"You have a great smile. You should smile more often."

"I smile a bunch. You just need to be around me more."

"Is that right? Maybe we can work on that?" Darlene smiled back.

After a few miles on the main highway, they approached an exit sign that pointed out their off-ramp. Juan decelerated, signaled the turn, and steered his car off the highway. A big brown sign noted "Park – 2 miles."

The last part of the drive was a scenic two-lane road, lined with trees. Juan had heard about this park from some of his coworkers, but hadn't seen it personally. He felt a slight nervous anticipation, like when opening a gift.

He expected a pleasant surprise, but didn't know exactly what he would find.

One last turn, and he could see the park downhill, a couple of hundred yards away. Several pavilions were clustered together on one side. The standard jungle gyms, softball backstops, and soccer goals were on the opposite side of the park. He saw just a handful of people in the park this Saturday morning, scattered about. Juan noticed a young man playing Frisbee catch with a golden retriever.

Juan smoothly steered his car into a parking space away from the other cars to give himself room to remove the picnic items.

Darlene got out, fairly skipped from the passenger side to the rear, and kissed Juan on the cheek before grabbing items.

The couple staked out a spot away from the paved parking lot. The grass was dewy, so Juan put down a plastic tarp then a blanket. Darlene watched the tarp then blanket unfold, then placed items on each of the four corners.

"I love this place. Good call on your part, Juan."

"Why, thank you, darling. Some of my coworkers have been out here before. They're the ones who told me about it. It's secluded enough, yet it's close to the highway. We definitely have to come out here again. Maybe when it gets warmer."

"You know it. Anyway, will you say grace please so we can start eating. I'm famished."

Juan took Darlene's hands into his, and asked God's blessing over the food. He could feel the warmth from her hands as she squeezed his hands.

After he finished the prayer, Darlene reached for plastic ware and passed a fork to Juan.

"What do ya have in this container?" he asked.

"Crab salad with peanut oil and a bit of soy sauce and wine vinegar. Hope you like it. There are some sandwiches and homemade chocolate chip cookies in there too. I know you missed a gym day to be with me, so I wanted to make it worth your while."

"Looks good, smells good. Let's do this, baby. Pass me a plate of that crab salad, please."

"Done." Darlene placed a couple of scoops of salad on his plate. "Here ya go."

Juan took a tentative bite, like he was the unwilling victim of a ghastly gastric experiment. His eyes widened and he emitted a low, "Mmmm."

"You like it?"

"Uhh, like it?" Juan looked at the remaining food on his plate. "No, I love it. This stuff is delicious," Juan answered while putting a second scoop of food into his mouth.

"Good, I hoped you would like it. Living by myself, I don't spend a lot of time in the kitchen. I did fret a bit over this because I wanted it to be tasty, while not wanting you to have the false impression that I'm little miss homemaker."

"Why are you worrying about that? You are an amazing lady, capable in so many different things. I had no doubt."

"Thanks. A girl always appreciates a heartfelt compliment."

The next couple of hours went well. The clouds got a bit thicker overhead, but the couple still enjoyed the seclusion. Juan's back up jacket idea came in handy as Darlene felt a chill from the damp breeze. He helped her get into the sleeves, and thought she looked adorable in his jacket. He hadn't felt this softness in his heart over a woman in a while. He could feel himself falling deeper and deeper for her, and didn't want to stop the fall.

As the conversation went on, Juan felt a drop of water hit his face. That drop was followed by another one, then a few more. Not a quick shower, but more like a mild drizzle started to leak from the clouds. They hurriedly gathered the food and utensils and hustled back to the car.

"We can spread out a blanket on the living room floor at my house and pretend like we're still outside. The day's not over."

"I like the way you think." The couple quickly loaded up the food and other items, and hastily walked over to Juan's car.

The drive back to Darlene's house seemed to go faster than the drive to the park. Not long after they were in Darlene's driveway, unloading the picnic items, Juan got a sense of being welcome, like being at home.

"You can leave it all in the kitchen for now while I get a quilt to spread out on the floor. Don't mind the mess, normally I keep it cleaner that this in here."

"Cleaner than this?" Juan asked. "It looks pretty much spotless to me. You sure you weren't a military drill instructor before?"

"Juan, you just gotta know where to look. Alright, the quilt is in place. Bring me some snacks, baby, then come over here and sit next to me."

Juan took off his shoes, placed them neatly at the door, then picked a parking spot in the middle of the floor. As he sat, he glanced around the room. There were the usual prints of outdoor scenes, mostly open fields with scattered trees, under mostly sunny skies. On the mantle, there were a few awards for civic involvement. On one wall hung a fairly large picture of Darlene and her parents. Her dad was a towering man with an open, friendly smile. Her mom was willowy and graceful-looking, beautiful as a swan.

"What drives you, Darlene? What makes you do what you do to help the community?"

"I never got a directive from God to follow in my parents' footsteps, but I saw the effect ministering to others can have on a community, regardless of where in the world you might be. I've had to evolve over the years. I tried to force the issue of trying to help when

I started out, but I think I get it more now. How about you? Have you thought about what God has in store for you? What he wants you to do with your days?"

Juan had to stop for a moment. He never really took the time to consider the fact that God had a plan for him. He mulled over an answer, maybe too long. "I will admit I haven't gone out of my way to seek God's direction, but..."

"That's ok," she said, halting him. "I'll bet he's been speaking to you all along. A little more work, and you'll hear His voice better. Once that happens, your life will never be the same. I guarantee you that."

Maybe now he had a bit more time to consider his response. That reprieve ended when he heard Darlene answer a phone call.

"Grant, wait...slow down...breathe first. Get a hold of yourself, then talk slowly. What happened to Grace? You say she's gone?" Darlene sighed heavily. "I'll be there as soon as I can." Darlene hung up and took Juan's hand, sensing he had started to tense up.

"Let me guess. The little princess has run away from home."

"Juan, don't be that way, baby. She left a note saying she'd only talk to me. I'm sorry, I can't leave her hanging. I have to go. Will you please take me home."

Juan averted his eyes from Darlene's gaze. "Yeah, whatever," he said in a perturbed tone.

Darlene softly caressed his face, and turned his chin. She looked into his eyes, looking for warmth. She saw a glint, but not a romantic one. The look from Juan was one of mounting frustration. She sensed it, and tried to soothe his feelings with a kiss. She didn't receive the same warmth she offered.

CHAPTER 33

Juan drove home in a frustrated mood. He thought he was falling in love with Darlene. Tough part was, one of the things about her he loved most was the very thing that got in his way when he wanted to be with her - her giving nature. He surmised that the way she reached out to people in need was never going to change. He started to wonder if their relationship would always be this way.

His cell phone rang. It was Dex. Of course at a time like this who else would it be but Dex. Juan could almost predict what Dex would say once he found out what was going on. Dex didn't disappoint.

"Juan, didn't I warn you, man? Women are what they are. You're never gonna change her. No use trying. Yeah, she's cool. Yeah, she's cute, but things are always gonna be this way."

"C'mon, Dex. You and I both know there are no absolutes."

"Some things, bro, are obvious. To her, you, at best, will be third in line. God comes first in her life. And, in no way am I saying she should put you ahead of God."

"Go ahead, say it. A combination of Grant and his daughter will be ahead of me."

"Well, yeah. But not in the way you think. I'm sure she told you that she isn't romantically interested in him. I have no doubt that's true. But what Grant stands for is what you can't overcome. He's a symbol of all those struggling in our society. He's a guy who needs help and Darlene can't resist the call to help."

"Nah, Dex. Darlene isn't that obsessed with him. She has balance. I would think she wouldn't let him or anyone else get in the way of a good relationship."

"Juan, women are different than men."

"You trying to be funny?"

"Not this time, bro. Even at her most logical, she can't help her nurturing nature. It just so happens Grant and his kid are on her radar. Question is, can you be the kind of man who can be faithful to a woman who is in love with a concept?"

"What do you mean?"

"Think about it. She has a concept, a view of who she is and how she operates. She also values the concept of serving the greater good. Think about it, seriously. Her forum with the paper gives her wide reach. She can share her concerns over a large area. She can also focus her concern, share it with others and get things solved. And, she can also put her effort where her mouth is. Not only can she remind others of civic responsibility, she can also make it personal. She writes it and lives it. She has the best of both worlds. Do you, brotha, have the patience to live a life where your woman is committed to things other than you?"

As much as he tried to resist, what Dex was saying got under his skin. Dex was right. What was he going to do? He was falling in love with Darlene. He wanted to be around her every day. He mulled over the situation, but he didn't pray. Maybe he should have.

Afternoon soon evolved into evening, and he hadn't heard from Darlene since she bolted from her apartment. He figured she got held up in all the drama, and he figured he wouldn't hear from her until late. In the midst of watching a ball game, his phone rang.

"Hello, boyfriend. It's your girlfriend."

"Hello to you, sweetie. How are things with Grace?"

"Man, let me tell ya. It was the weirdest thing. She wrote a note in this cryptic, overly dramatic language, said she was running away. Grant was frantic. Just so happens she was down the street at the neighborhood park. She wasn't in danger. It was more like she was jerking her dad's chain. If it wasn't so mean, it would almost be funny. It took Grant an hour after her return for his blood pressure to come down. You should've seen him, pacing and wringing his hands. Hey, are you okay?" Darlene stared and asked Juan. "Even though I've been babbling, I sense you're not with me on this."

"Guess I didn't hide it so well. Can I ask you something?"

"You can ask me anything, baby."

"How do you see me fitting in your life? "

"Are you asking me if I'm willing to change? Juan, you know me a bit. You see my life, what's important to me."

"Darlene, just the nature of us dating means that things are different than they were before we met. I'm changing, evolving. Before you, I didn't have to think about anyone else. Didn't even want to some days. Now, you're always on my mind. Am I the same to you?

"We all change, whether we want to or not. Are you concerned that I will drop you every time a crisis comes up?"

"I wouldn't say that. But to answer your question, yes, I am a bit concerned," Juan admitted.

"Alright. I see it. Jealous and insecure, still." Darlene sighed, loud enough for Juan to hear. "Look. I don't want to lead you on. I'm falling in love with you, Juan, I really am. But, there are concerns in my spirit that won't let me sit still. If a man can deal with that and stand by my side, I can make it worth his while."

"What do you mean by *worth his while*? You can refer to me directly, unless there's some other guy out there, like Grant for instance."

"Juan, don't play dumb. You know what I mean. No other man is competing for your spot in my heart. There are things I need from my man, and I'm not talking sexual. I'm talking about honesty, love support, companionship, and friendship. You and I could have a great relationship, the way God intends. All you gotta do is get in tune with His will for your life, then you'll see."

"You say you're falling in love with me, but yet you run away from me to see about some other guy and his problems? Look, I'm not throwing a fit about this, but honestly, from the outside looking in, it doesn't seem to match up."

"Juan, this isn't the sixties. Women today don't just sit around waiting for men to come see about them. This world is busted and broken. In some small way, I have been blessed to do something about the things that trouble me. Broken homes. Discouraged souls. People wandering away from God. Some who don't even realize they're disconnected from the Lord. If God puts it on your heart to walk alongside me as I do His will, what we can have can be sweet. If that isn't on your heart, if that kind of life doesn't interest you..."

"Oh, so now if this doesn't work out between us, it's gonna be on me? I sit here and wait for you while you run off to see about some other guy, but the possibility of our relationship failing is my fault? I certainly don't understand that."

Although Juan expressed himself in a near monotone manner, Darlene received his words as if they were tinged with anger. She worked hard to catch herself, catch her emotions, tried to reason through her head to come up with words that would resonate with Juan. She found herself at a loss.

"Now suddenly you're all quiet. You make a living based on the words you choose. Now, when I need to hear something encouraging from you, you're speechless?" Juan said with a note of frustration resonating in his voice.

"Maybe we should take some time to pray and contemplate this. Figure out what the right way ahead is for us. Let the emotions fade before we say anything else."

"I don't need to pray or meditate to know I want you in my life, Darlene."

"Look, things are just crazy now. I'm sorry, but I need a couple of days to think over everything. Maybe you do as well. I really do care about you, but I need time. We'll talk soon. Bye, Juan." She hung up before he could respond.

Juan sat on his easy chair in a stunned state. What had just happened? "Did we just break up?" he wondered aloud. "She hung up with no word of romantic intimacy," he muttered. What kind of point was she trying to leave with him? She "cared" about him? One cares about a pet or a cause. What happened to the love she offered?

CHAPTER 34

The next few days were brutal for Juan. He and Darlene hadn't spoken at all since their argument. Darlene had become a special part of his life. Now, just like that, she was gone and much too fast for him to figure out what had happened that was irreversible.

When Sunday came and went and he didn't see Darlene at church, he knew that things between them had probably come to an end. For the first time in a long time, his desire for logic and order were completely worthless. He hadn't felt this helpless and confused in a long while. *If this is love*, Juan thought, *I don't know if the pain is worth it.*

She didn't return his phone calls, his email messages, nothing. The next couple of Sundays, Juan didn't go to church. He cared too much for Darlene to put her in an awkward position of seeing him if she really didn't want to be around him. He talked to Dex about it, and surprisingly for a change, Dex actually had something more heartfelt than the usual player attitude and perspective. He was actually somewhat supportive and mature when discussing Darlene's attitude.

Juan may have known Darlene for just a few short months, but her suddenly distancing herself punched a jagged hole in his heart and he had no idea how to patch it. He thought only her affection would fill it.

When he felt he had exhausted all he knew to consider, he broke down and got on his knees. His attempt at prayer started out with the usual clichés of *thee* and *thou*. After a few unsatisfactory moments down that path, Juan stopped and collected himself.

"Jesus, I need your help. I don't know what to do about Darlene. I don't know what to do about me. But, I do know you can guide me through this weird, dark time in my life. I ask you to look after Darlene. She is a special lady with a big heart for you. She wants to serve you with all of her heart. Please, God. Give her what she needs to continue in your will.

"Also, Lord, for the two of us, I ask that you make clear the way ahead. Please let us both know what we need to be aware of between one another. I do love her, or at least I think I do. I want to treat her right. Maybe you don't have this in store for us, or for us right now. Please clear things up between us so there is no unnecessary emotion or confusion.

"Most of all, Lord, I pray for me. I have been adrift for so long. I haven't turned my life over to you like I should. I haven't asked you to lead me day by day, moment by moment. Now, I understand, a little bit anyway. You are in charge. I wish to serve you, in whatever way you choose."

Juan stayed on his knees for a while. He asked God to burn brighter in his life, and to provide that clarity in everyday events so he wouldn't doubt or question his choices.

As he got up from off his knees, his spirit sensed a level of calm such as he'd never felt before. The phone rang. Caller ID noted it was Darlene.

"Hi," he said, sounding melancholy when he answered.

"Hi. How are you?" Darlene sounded rather forlorn in her response.

"I'm good, but I do have to admit that in our last conversation I heard a different part of you that I really didn't expect."

"Listen, Juan, I was being honest, that's all. I thought you were man enough to handle me being frank. What tripped you up?"

"Tripped me up? Nah, it wasn't like that at all. To me, it sounded like you needed me to evolve. I'm gonna do that, just not on your timing. I'm not going to sit back while you nurse the next guy's wounds."

"I wasn't nursing anyone's wounds. I was doing what I believe God wanted me to do. If you're doing what God tells you to do, the timing will be right-on. And don't try to make this about Grant because it's not."

Juan took a pause, and took an audible sigh, but didn't say anything.

"What was that for? Are you frustrated with me?" she asked, hearing his discontent over the phone.

"To answer your question, yeah, I am frustrated. I'm frustrated about how quickly everything changed. Suddenly, we can't come to an agreement on something that seems workable? As for Grant, I could care less about the next dude. I'm talking about us, Darlene. I know I have a ways to go in my walk with God. I understand that. But I'm willing. I'm open to being a better me. As for our relationship, I thought what we had was workable."

"Workable to whom, exactly, Juan? For me to place my trust in you, I need to know your level of commitment to me and most definitely to God. I don't want to find out later into our relationship that we really weren't on the same level, faith-wise. The incident with Grant does make me wonder how much you really do know me. What it amounts to is a matter of trust, something I don't think you have."

Juan took another pause, as if he were frantically searching for something to say.

"You keep going quiet on me. This caught you off guard, didn't it?" Darlene asked.

"You want everything to be about you, Darlene. That's what it seems like to me. You won't admit that maybe, just maybe you could be wrong. Yet, when it comes to me, you expect me to be a fully-formed Christian, right out the box, when you aren't one either. You let one disagreement over another guy lead to all of this? Come on now, Darlene."

"Hold up, Juan. First of all, I never said I was fully formed. Yeah, I'm still in need of spiritual growth. I understand that. But I don't think I would be jealous or angry if you were reaching out to help someone in trouble. But obviously you can't deal with a woman like me."

It was Darlene's turn to take a pause. The quiet hung on the air for a few seconds, but it seemed to both of them like it lasted much longer.

Darlene broke the silence. "Look, Juan, I feel we could have the potential to make some good things happen. But now, I just don't know if the time is right."

"And you're the only one who gets to decide? What about my thoughts on that?"

"I've heard everything you've said and what you didn't say, too. And no, you don't have to throw out a last-ditch 'but I love you' to keep things going. Let me say it again. Maybe the time isn't right for us."

"And I say, maybe you need to have more patience. Maybe you should try looking at things from my perspective," Juan shot back.

"Maybe I should. But I don't have the patience right now, and I don't want to keep going back and forth with you over the same issues." As soon as Darlene said it, she immediately regretted her words. Even though the words weren't that harsh, the effect on the conversation was immediate. There was nothing left to offer after that.

"Well, I guess you got me in check. I don't have any other response. I'm not big on apologies, but for what it's worth, I'm sorry. It looks like we'll never know how good we could have been."

"Don't say that. It sounds like you're pouting."

"And you sound like you're looking to shut us down. That's cool, though. I'm not one to beg. So..."

"So, I guess we should take some time to rethink what we're thinking and saying. I'm gonna let you go. Take care, Juan. God bless you. I mean it."

"Yeah, you too, Darlene. You too."

As Juan hung up, he felt a hollow feeling in the pit of his stomach. If it was a shut-down, it wasn't nearly as violent as the breakups he heard about as a kid. But, in this case, it still hurt. He didn't feel that Darlene tried to understand his position at all. He didn't deny any of his shortcomings, but he felt he still took a big hit. *I'm not the guy I'm destined to be*, he thought. *Why was she so quick to derail things?*

CHAPTER 35

Weeks had elapsed since Juan's last phone conversation with Darlene. Things ended and ended badly. Emotions ran high and deep. Both Darlene and Juan tried hard to not say things that were intentionally inflammatory, but what was said still hurt. The goodbye at the end of the conversation possessed what Juan took as a tone of finality. He constantly replayed their conversation in his head in the following weeks.

In a literal sense, he didn't see any of the things he said then as rude or unfair. He had to also admit that the things Darlene said were fair and true to God and His will. In earlier years, he might have felt like he was completely in the right at the end. This time, he was more baffled than anything else. How could two people who claimed they loved God and loved each other not find common ground to continue in a relationship? What happened? Juan had no answer, and that fact dug at him like a dull knife.

He found himself not sleeping well, and not nearly as focused in any part of his life. This particular morning, like most, he was wide awake before his alarm went off. Too alert to rest, too tired to get out of bed with a chipper attitude.

The alarm went off, and Juan rolled over to shut it off. He looked at the clock, and released a sigh.

Since it was Saturday, it was early gym day. He got up, shuffled sleepily through a quick shower and donned some workout clothes. As he loaded a change of clothes into his gym bag, his phone rang. *Dex*, Juan thought. *Who else would call this time of morning?*

"Juan, let's go to work. The gym calls, bro."

"I'm in. Gotta have it, and you know it's true. I'll see you in about half an hour."

"You got it."

Juan got dressed and headed to the gym and right away he started his routine workout on the treadmill. Dex showed up shortly thereafter.

"How you doing, bro?" Juan asked Dex when he saw him after getting off the treadmill.

"I'm good, bro. Question is, how are you, and tell me the truth. Remember, this is Dex you're talking to.

Juan and Dex talked as they walked toward the men's locker room.

"I'm good, man."

"I gotta admit, you do seem to be holding up well. Better than I would be, given how much you cared about your girl. Knowing me, I'd be out in the clubs working hard trying to forget a lady like Darlene."

"Yeah, but what are you gonna do? I'm thankful to God that He's giving me the stuff to get through the day. Do I miss her? Yeah, every moment, every day. But God is good. I have all I need. Today is a blessing. And as for Darlene, I'm sure she's doing well. I don't hate her or any other woman who I'm not with any more."

"You're not just saying all this to convince yourself or convince me, are you?"

Juan took in a deep breath and waited a couple of beats to accentuate his point. "No. I'm not at a point where I have to convince anyone. I know some of the things I didn't do with Darlene that might have made things better, or maybe even helped us recover when things got crazy and out of hand. In some ways, I know that I'm part of the reason that caused our relationship not to work out. But, the sun is out today. We move ahead."

"Sure thing. So since you're moving, move back to the gym floor," Dex said jokingly.

"Yeah, let's do this."

Juan thought about his words to Dex. He actually wasn't trying to convince Dex or himself of anything. In other years, that would have been the case. He used to believe strongly in saving face and image above all else. Now, he had a better sense of what God was trying to do in his spirit. Juan looked forward to what God would show him, what God would walk him through in life. The future looked promising.

THE END

DISCUSSION QUESTIONS

1. What do you think is the significance of the novel's title, *None of Our Hands Are Clean*?
2. What message do you think this novel conveys? Explain.

3. How is God's influence shown in the story?

4. Does this book relate to today's way of handling relationships? How?

5. What do you like/dislike about Juan? Why?

6. What do you like/dislike about Darlene? Why?

7. Is Dex a true friend to Juan? Why or why not?

8. What do you think of Darlene and Grant's relationship?

9. What do you think about the relationship between Juan and Darlene?

10. How authentic is the culture or era represented in "None of Our Hands Are Clean"?

ABOUT THE AUTHOR

Ralph Thompson, Jr. was born and reared in Memphis, Tennessee. He accepted Christ in April of 1976. Since then, he's been on this journey of life. After a 26-year career in the U.S. Air Force and Air Force Reserve, he came home to serve. Whether it's at his church, Mt. Vernon Baptist Church, or Alpha Delta Lambda chapter of Alpha Phi Alpha Fraternity, Incorporated, Thompson works alongside like-minded folks in community uplift. In his spare time, Thompson enjoys reading, classic film, music, travel, and long debates about issues. None of Our Hands Are Clean is his first published novel.

To arrange speaking engagements, book signings
and author appearances
Email - Ralph Thompson, Jr.
Navgator17@yahoo.com
www.facebook.com/RalphThompsonJr
Twitter: @SomRandomOlDude
LinkedIn: Ralph Thompson, Jr.